'What Do You Want?'

'You.'

He whispered it so softly, she was afraid she was going to cry. And that he would misunderstand her tears. 'You're going to be disappointed.'

'Shh.' He placed his finger to her lips. He wanted no protests, no disclaimers. He only wanted her. 'Let me be the judge of that.'

Moved by instincts, by an overwhelming need to connect, Fiona pressed her lips to the finger he held against them. She saw a strange look enter his eyes. A look that was equal parts tender and passionate and left her instantly weak.

Fiona's head began to spin. Just for now, just for this evening, she would delude herself. She would pretend that this was not a one-time thing, but something that was the beginning of forever.

The way she fervently wished it was.

Dear Reader

This month in Desire™ we're delighted to be able to introduce you to some sensational new mini-series! Top author Marie Ferrarella brings us the first of five books about **The Cutler Family**. Henry Cutler and Fiona Reilly don't get off to a good start when he turns up at her house with flowers—and she mistakes him for the delivery man! But by the time he proposes, she's ready to join the Cutler clan.

The Rulebreakers kicks off with a sexy millionaire, Joe Caruthers, who has it all—success, wealth, good looks—but will a baby fit into his future plans? And in **The McCloud Brides**, Jesse Barrister returns home to claim the son he never knew...and another night in Mandy McCloud's arms.

Our hunky **Man of the Month** is Jordan Westcott, a tycoon who goes undercover in his family firm…only to walk into the lair of stubborn beauty Mistral St. Michel.

Finally, Nancy Martin is back with an **Opposites Attract** story. And Patty Salier's heroine joins a dating agency—that *guarantees* marriage!

Happy reading

The Editors

Fiona and the Sexy Stranger

MARIE FERRARELLA

SILHOUETTE

DESIRE®

To Lucy Tscherne,
with love for a faithful friendship

*Silhouette, Silhouette Desire and Colophon
are registered trademarks of Harlequin Books S.A.,
used under licence.*

*First published in Great Britain 1999
Silhouette Books, Eton House, 18-24 Paradise Road,
Richmond, Surrey TW9 1SR*

© Marie Rydzynski-Ferrarella 1998

ISBN 0 373 52071 9

22-9905

*Printed and bound in Spain
by Litografia Rosés S.A., Barcelona*

From the author

Dearest Reader,

One of the questions people always ask is 'Where do you get your ideas?' My standard answer is 'Life,' which people take to mean that I'm being cleverly secretive and refusing to answer. Well, my answer stands, but I can be more specific if you like. Take *Fiona And The Sexy Stranger*. The heroine's name (and *only* her name) belongs to one of the check-out girls at my favourite supermarket. I fell in love with her name and decided then and there to use the name in a book at the first opportunity. Okay, so where's the story?

Well, the idea for how she and the hero meet happened in a roundabout way to me. I came home one day to find a perfectly stunning résumé for a physicist lying beside my fax machine. My husband's a physicist, but since the names were different, and I know his every move, I knew the résumé wasn't his. I called said résumé sender and told his answering machine that since I was a writer, and, in any case, already had my very own physicist, I had no openings for him. I wished him luck elsewhere. I never met the man, but then I started thinking, what if…? That's all it takes. What if…? The brain is a wonderful instrument. It just needs a little greasing, and off it goes. While mine was going off, creating Fiona and Henry's story, Henry suddenly got a family and you, dearest reader, suddenly got the first book of a mini-series.

And *that's* how it works. Hope you like it.

Love,

Marie Ferrarella

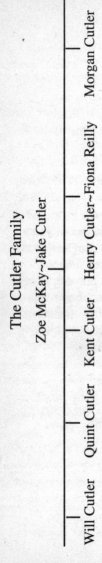

The Cutler Family

Zoe McKay~Jake Cutler

Will Cutler   Quint Cutler   Kent Cutler   Henry Cutler~Fiona Reilly   Morgan Cutler

1

Fiona Reilly stared at the piece of paper in her hand. Unlike the others, this one had nothing to do with confirmation of a hundred guinea hens, or an order for four dozen long-stemmed wineglasses. It wasn't even yet another change in plans for the Kellerman wedding that was scheduled for three weeks from Saturday and was destined to drive her out of her mind if Mr. and Mrs. Kellerman didn't finally make up theirs. So far, there had been no less than fifteen such communications between the Kellermans and the fax line designated for her business.

No, this piece of paper, found nestled in the center of the half dozen other sheets that had been spewed out by her fax machine, was extolling the qualifications, experience and educational background of one Henry Cutler.

It was a résumé. A rather impressive résumé, Fiona thought as she scanned it quickly, belonging to a man who had amassed a number of awards in the advertising field. A résumé that had somehow lost its way and wound up in the wrong place.

"Montana?" she murmured under her breath as

she noted where he had gone to school and most recently worked. "I didn't know they needed to advertise anything in Montana, did you, Velcro?"

In response to her question, the calico-colored Persian cat she'd chosen to name Velcro—for reasons that became obvious to even the most casual of observers after a few minutes in the cat's presence—leaped up on her lap and immediately made herself comfortable. Fiona knew better than to try to push her off.

As she ran her fingers over Velcro's fur, Fiona's first instinct was just to shrug off the error and toss the résumé away. The last thing she needed was more paper cluttering up the already-cluttered area of her kitchen that she had set aside as her office. But as she began to crumple up the résumé, Velcro raised her head and looked at her accusingly. Fiona knew it was just because she'd stopped petting the cat, but the look in Velcro's eyes had repercussions.

"Yeah, maybe you're right." She stopped crumpling.

On the heels of her impulse came the inevitable twinge of conscience. The same conscience that kept her from stepping on bugs or squashing spiders, no matter how hairy, that skittered across her path.

Sighing, she placed the sheet on top of the others and smoothed it out. Velcro voiced her complaint at sharing the space with an indignant little "meow" and dug her claws in just far enough to get a firm hold on Fiona's jeans. Accustomed to Velcro's tenacious habits, Fiona hardly noticed.

What she did notice was that there was no line in the résumé that testified to Henry's being currently employed. He wasn't looking to change jobs, he needed one. Her vivid imagination conjured up a mental picture of the man sitting by the phone, waiting for a reply that would never come because she had gotten his résumé by mistake.

That settled it. She put thoughts of her work on hold as she twisted in her chair to reach for the telephone. Velcro voiced another rather strong protest over the sudden shift.

"If you don't like it, you can always get off," Fiona told the cat. Velcro seemed to raise a disdainful eye in her direction, but remained firmly entrenched exactly where she was. Though she tried to act aloof, beneath the disdain was a cat who craved companionship. "No, I didn't think so."

Her eyes on the second line of the résumé, Fiona tapped out the numbers to Henry's telephone. It rang three times. On the fourth ring, the receiver was picked up.

"Hi," the voice on the other end drawled. It was deep and resonant, filling the phone with a rush of pure male sexuality with just a single word.

Collecting herself, Fiona said quickly, "Hello, you don't know me, but—"

"This is Henry Cutler," the voice informed her in the same laid-back tone that Fiona found arousing at the same time that it was soothing.

She didn't realize she was petting Velcro so hard

until the cat meowed a loud protest. "Yes, I know, I was just calling to—"

"—I can't come to the phone right now, but if you leave your name and number, I'll be sure to get back to you."

An answering machine. Fiona stared at the receiver in mute disbelief. The voice on the other end had sounded to laid-back, so gut-level melodic and sexual, she hadn't realized that she was talking to a recording. Feeling foolish now, she recovered just as the beep sounded. Her mind scrambled, trying to form a coherent message.

"This is Fiona Reilly. You don't know me, but you sent a copy of your résumé to my fax machine. It's a very nice résumé, and while I'd love to hire you, I don't think working for a tiny company just getting its feet solidly planted on the ground is what you had in mind when you sent the résumé. I'd suggest that you resend your résumé and this time be a little bit more careful where your fingers do the walking."

The click on the other end told her that she'd used up her allotted space and ended her message just in time. Satisfied she'd done her good deed, Fiona hung up. And then a lazy smile drifted over her lips as she replayed his outgoing message in her mind. God, but that man did have one hell of a sexy voice.

Stroking the cat, she closed her eyes, letting the memory of the voice drift over her. Deep, resonant and incredibly sensual, it had wound its way through her system, curling her toes. She sank deeper into the soft leather chair and sighed.

What did a man with a voice like that look like?

The question no sooner occurred to her than Fiona began answering it. With very little effort at all, she gave Henry Cutler broad shoulders, slender, tapering hips, a killer smile and deep, chestnut brown hair that insisted on being the slightest bit unruly. It curled wantonly, just enough to make a woman's fingers itch.

She rubbed her palm along Velcro's back. The cat purred contentedly. The purr vibrated through the animal's body, joining with her hand. The sensation slowly traveled up her arm until it managed to mushroom throughout her entire body.

Fiona savored the feeling and the image for a long moment, then roused herself.

It was a nice daydream. Reality was that Henry Cutler was probably five foot three, barrel-chested with a fifty-three-inch waist and spindly legs. Daydreams were always infinitely better than reality, she mused. They were also a lot safer.

Enough of a break, she told herself, it was time to get back to work. Her business wasn't about to run itself.

She scooped Velcro up and deposited the protesting cat on the floor, then moved in closer to her desk. There was a mountain of papers to sort through. Fiona placed the résumé to one side, for the moment letting it sit in its own singular pile. As soon as she did, she saw the page that was behind it. A quick read had her stifling an involuntary groan. It was another missive from Mrs. Kellerman about the upcoming wedding. Chicken Kiev was out, lobster bisque was now in.

Mrs. Kellerman had changed the menu. Again. Fiona could feel several of her hairs turning gray at the roots. Wouldn't it be nice, she mused, if that sexy stranger was actually Prince Charming and could whisk her away from wicked witches like Mrs. Kellerman? Only thing was, she'd have to have a sexier name to call him than Henry. Fiona grinned to herself. It was always something, wasn't it?

The small kitchen was alive with a combination of aromas guaranteed to make both boys and men drool and beg for a taste. Unlike the rest of the house, which existed in haphazard clutter and whose only pattern was early, comfortable chaos, the kitchen, though compact in size, was state of the art. As soon as the business had begun earning a little money, Fiona had funneled it all back in and built her kitchen according to utilitarian requirements. She wanted and got only the best. The kitchen was where she spent a great deal of her time and it was the hub for the foundation of her ever-growing reputation.

Ever since she'd catered her first party as a favor for a friend who had a penchant for burning even water, Fiona's company had been climbing steadily up the hill of success. She wouldn't be satisfied until she claimed the flag at the top.

Bridgette Turner frowned at her younger sister

over the row of cream puffs she was packing. No one made cream puffs like Fiona. They all but floated into the box, backing up Fiona's claim that they were almost lighter than air.

Lighter than air. Just like Fiona's brain, Bridgette thought in exasperated annoyance. For such a sweet-tempered little thing, her sister could be maddeningly stubborn at times. Like now.

She slid the lid over the cream puffs. "But why won't you at least come and meet Brian's friend? An innocent little dinner, what harm is there in that?"

An innocent little dinner, Bridgette added silently, that she had gone through great lengths to arrange. Fiona spent so much time mothering this fledgling catering company of hers, she spent absolutely no time on, and certainly seemed to have no interest in, her social life. Someone had to look out for her before she wound up old and alone, still making cream puffs.

Fiona spared her sister a look as she quickly scanned her checklist for the Kellerman wedding a fourth time. She couldn't wait for this day to be over with.

"The harm, Bridgette, will be to me and my intestinal tract after I spend half the night in your bathroom, retching."

Bridgette knew it wasn't an egotistical slur aimed at her cooking, even though she didn't hold a candle to Fiona when it came to preparing anything remotely fancy. Fiona's objection was far more fundamental than that and all the more frustrating for it.

"You're a grown woman, Fiona," Bridgette reminded her, even though she was trying to bully Fiona into letting her arrange her life.

Knowing she had no intentions of letting Bridgette win this argument no matter what was said, Fiona began packing the guinea hens that had been Mrs. Kellerman's final choice as of three-thirty yesterday.

"Yes, and as a grown woman, I should be able to make up my mind as to whom I choose to socialize with."

"Socialize?" Bridgette hooted. She opened another box and continued to pack cream puffs. "Ghosts have a more social life than you do."

Fiona arched an eyebrow. Why did Bridgette always pick the worst times to play matchmaker? Then she shrugged inwardly. She supposed that wasn't strictly true. There was never a good time to have her sister play matchmaker.

"I see a lot of people," she informed Bridgette coolly, her fingers flying as she made the transfer from baking pan to padded box.

"In the line of duty," Bridgette observed pointedly. No one could match Fiona when it came to people skills. On a work-related level. One-to-one on a personal basis was something else again. Something she repeatedly shied away from. "Oh, you're a charming bit of a thing, you are." Bridgette mimicked their grandmother's thick brogue to a tee, succeeding in coaxing a smile out of Fiona. "Flitting from one person to the other, one man to the other." Bridgette's brogue vanished as she leveled an accusing look at her sister. "As long as it's just business you're talking about."

Fiona picked up the brogue. "In case you haven't noticed, Bridgette, me darlin', it's a business I'm supposed to be runnin'." She dropped it again, because this was important to her and too serious to joke about. "My business, which I'm trying very hard to get to take off. That kind of thing won't happen if I spend my time going out with every Tom, Dick or Harry."

She closed the lid with finality. Moving the box aside, she opened another. Everything had to be perfect. There were three more daughters in the wings, separated by two years apiece. If she impressed Mr. and Mrs. Kellerman today, Fiona felt confident she would secure at least three more catering affairs in the future. Perhaps even more from the guests.

If she survived this one.

Bridgette gave a very unladylike snort. "I'd settle for you going out with a single Tom or Dick *or* Harry. Or an Alfred," she added, referring to the man she had persuaded her husband, after much wheedling, to invite over for dinner tonight. Brian had the same maddening philosophy as Fiona—he wanted things to happen "naturally." As if the big jerk actually believed that their own meeting had happened "naturally," when it was only after a great deal of effort on her part, thank-you-very-much.

Bridgette looked at Fiona pointedly. "Fiona, you're not getting any younger."

Fiona stopped packing. Of the two of them, Bridgette had always been the family pride and joy. The one the boys had all flocked to when both of them were growing up. The one in whose shadow she had always stood, proud to be her sister and relieved to have a shadow to take refuge in. Not for her was the awkwardness of trying to make small talk while her whole mind had gone completely blank and her tongue had turned to shoe leather.

"You make it sound as if I've got one foot in the grave. I'm only twenty-six, Bridgette." She went back to work. Time was at a premium and growing short. "Although I must admit that talking to you is aging me rapidly."

Bridgette played the last card in her depleted hand. "Just say you'll come to dinner and I'll stop talking, I promise."

Glancing up, Fiona saw that Bridgette had one hand raised as if she were taking a solemn oath before a judge. She laughed softly. "Tempting as that is, I can't. I've got work to do."

The phone rang, but Bridgette ignored it as she struggled not to shout at her sister. "You've got work to hide behind."

Fiona wiped her hands on the towel she had slung over one shoulder. "Saved by the bell," she said brightly, terminating, she hoped, the discussion. Reaching for the wall phone, she fervently prayed it wasn't Mrs. Kellerman with a last-minute change.

"Painless Parties," Fiona announced into the receiver. "Catering to suit your every whim and requirement. This is Fiona Reilly, how may I help you?''

For a moment there was only silence on the other end.

Fiona frowned, unwilling to hang up and make herself the target for more of Bridgette's nagging and cajoling. ''Hello?''

Bridgette looked up, mildly interested. ''If it's an obscene caller, don't hang up,'' she instructed. ''You need the practice.''

Fiona waved an annoyed hand at her sister. ''Hello?'' she repeated. ''Is anyone there?''

''Are you the woman who called me about my misdirected résumé?'' the voice on the other end asked.

He didn't have to say who he was. Even if he hadn't mentioned the résumé, Fiona would have recognized the drawl instantly. Though she'd made the call over three weeks ago, the voice, and the fantasy she'd built around it, had remained with her for a while and now vividly sprang forth at the sound of his voice.

''Henry?''

Out of the corner of her eye, she saw that Bridgette had stopped packing the last of the cream puffs. Instantly alert, her face was alive with questions. Fiona deliberately turned her back on her sister. There was going to be the devil to pay as soon as she hung up.

Her guess as to his identity was rewarded with a deep chuckle that undulated along her body, unsettling her in all sorts of delicious ways she meant to mentally record and savor when she wasn't under Bridgette's intense scrutiny.

"How did you know?" His voice curled around each syllable.

"I recognized your voice from your answering machine. Besides, it's not every day I get a résumé lodged in between my order for a hundred guinea hens and a request for lobster bisque."

This time the pause on the other end was shorter. "Excuse me?"

"I run a catering business," she explained. She vaguely wondered if the drawl meant that he was also slow on the uptake. She'd mentioned the name of her catering company before she'd even said her name.

A short laugh warmed her ear. "Oh, that's the kind of parties you meant."

Fiona struggled not to sink into the sound. "Yes, why? What did you think I meant?"

He laughed again, this time more heartily. She realized he'd totally misunderstood her meaning about catering to whims and needs.

"Never mind, doesn't matter. Listen, the reason I'm calling is to tell you that they hired me a couple of weeks ago."

It didn't occur to her to ask why he felt that he had to call her with this information. She was genuinely happy that she'd managed, in a small way, to help. "Congratulations."

She sounded as if she meant it, Hank Cutler thought, gripping the receiver. Which made what he was about to say even easier and more important to him. He was a man who always paid his debts, no matter how large or small. This, he reasoned, was a large one.

"I figure if it hadn't been for you taking pity on a stranger whose fingers are too thick to hit the right numbers, I'd still be sitting here in my living room, wondering if Collins Walker was ever going to call me in for an interview."

His gratitude pleased her no end, but Fiona played down her role in his success. "I didn't do anything except call you."

"Oh, but that was a very important call and I'd just like to express my gratitude."

"All right." Fiona paused, waiting for him to say something else, perhaps launch into a lengthier thank-you. Fiona couldn't think of anything else to say but she silently hoped Henry would carry the conversational ball. She would have been willing to sit and listen to him read the phone book just to hear the sound of his voice a little longer.

"Where would you like to go?" he asked.

Had she missed a step? Fiona turned again because a very curious Bridgette had stopped packing altogether and was now almost in her face, her lips forming the word "who" over and over again like a determined owl. Fiona waved her sister back to the counter and the cream puffs. Much as she wanted to continue to listen to Henry's voice, she had to get going soon.

"Excuse me?"

"I'd like to say thanks over dinner," he clarified. "As you probably can guess if you looked at my résumé, I'm new around these parts. Where's the best place to eat?"

"My kitchen." The reply came automatically. Fiona was confident about very little when it came to herself, but she had no doubts about her ability to produce minor miracles in the kitchen.

The laugh came again, seducing her. "Is that anything like a busman's holiday?"

It took her a moment to rouse herself and to make sense of his question. "No, wait, I didn't mean that the way it sounded." Fiona prayed he hadn't thought she was inviting him over. The fantasy vanished in a large puff of smoke.

"How did you mean it?" Hank drawled gamely, wondering what had produced the change in her voice. She sounded almost nervous now.

"I mean, I never go out to eat. I'm too busy."

"Couldn't you make a little time?" he coaxed. She had him curious now. "I chew faster than I talk."

Fiona could feel her palms growing damp around the receiver. Damn it, he wasn't even in the room. Why was she having this absolutely ridiculous reaction? Was she always going to be doomed to feel this way every time a conversation threatened to become personal?

Fiona heard Bridgette clear her throat. She stiffened her back. She could almost feel the darts Bridgette's eyes were throwing her way. Ignoring them, she dealt with the immediate threat at her door—or her phone—as best she could. At this rate, she was going to be emotionally drained before she ever got to the Kellerman house.

"I'm sure you can, Henry, but that still doesn't change the fact that I am very, very busy. This is June and I've got six weddings to do in the next three weeks. I really don't have any time to spare." Her voice was picking up speed like an untended car parked uphill in San Francisco whose brakes had just given way.

"I really would like to express my gratitude somehow," he insisted.

Even insisting took on new ramifications when spoken in a voice that was richer than molasses pouring out of a container in a warm climate. She struggled not to allow herself to drown in the sound.

"You already did. You said thank you," she noted.

Bridgette was now circling her like a shark looking for a way into the diver's steel protective cage. Each time Fiona turned, Bridgette moved with her, gesturing madly. Fiona felt as if she was being laid siege to from without and within.

"Now I really have to go. Good luck with your job, Henry." She hung up quickly before he could say anything further and weaken her shaky ramparts even more than they already were.

Fiona looked up to see Bridgette glaring at her. If looks could kill, this would have been the last wedding she was destined to cater.

Bridgette could barely contain her annoyance. "Did you just hang up on a man?"

Passing her on her way back to the counter and the unpacked guinea hens, Fiona shrugged. "Sure looks that way."

Bridgette felt like hitting her head against the wall. Better yet, she felt like hitting Fiona's head against the wall. "A man who wanted to take you out?"

Fiona sighed. Why couldn't Bridgette just drop it and get back to work? "It's all very platonic. He didn't want to take *me* out, Bridgette. He just wanted to say thank-you."

Bridgette crossed her arms, waiting for an explanation. None was forthcoming. "For?"

Fiona blew out a breath. Bridgette was going to make a big deal of this, she just knew it. Bridgette could make a big deal out of the box boy offering to help Fiona out of the supermarket with an overloaded cart. Never mind that she always tipped him well for his services.

"For calling him because he'd accidentally sent his résumé here instead of to some advertising firm."

Bridgette looked at the wall phone with renewed awe and interest. "That was Mr. Sexiest-Voice-In-The-Whole-World?"

Fiona bitterly regretted ever saying that to Bridgette. It had been in a moment of weakness and she should have had her mouth taped because of it. But who had expected the man to suddenly surface in her life?

Sighing, she nodded. "Yes."

Bridgette looked toward the fax machine that was perched on the battered desk Fiona had rescued from a garage sale.

"You still have his résumé?"

"It's around here somewhere." Too late, she realized she shouldn't have said that. She had an awful feeling. Fiona knew that tone. Bridgette was going to call Cutler and beg him to reconsider taking her out. Fiona wouldn't have put it past her. "Look, we are up to our ears in guinea hens, Bridgette. Now if you're going to help me, help me, don't talk nonsense about looking at some résumé. I've got thirty-five more of these little birds to pack. And, unless you know some magic trick to make them hop into the boxes themselves, I suggest you start herding them into their proper places."

Bridgette slanted her sister a disgusted look. "You're hopeless, you know that?"

She'd heard all this before and more than once. You'd think Bridgette would get tired of saying it. "I'm happy the way I am."

Bridgette looked at the guinea hens they'd spent an hour dressing this morning. "What, playing dress-up with chickens?"

"No, making something of myself. Getting a business started. A good business." Her chin went up, defying a man who no longer existed. "Dad never thought I'd amount to anything."

Gregarious and outgoing to the outside world, Shawn Reilly had turned a different face toward his family. Especially when he felt displeased. And he had never been pleased with Fiona.

"Dad was an idiot. God rest his soul," Bridgette tacked on mechanically.

Relenting, Bridgette decided to leave Fiona alone for the time being. She had a lot on her mind. But as soon as she could, Bridgette promised herself that she was going to hunt up both that résumé and Mr. Sexiest-Voice-In-The-Whole-World. Fiona would thank her for it. Eventually.

2

─────►◄─────

He'd never believed in letting debts pile up. It didn't matter if it was monetary or a debt of the spirit, a debt had to be paid. And quickly, if possible.

It was something that Henry Cutler—Hank, to his friends—assumed had been taught to him by one of his parents, but was so ingrained in his nature that it seemed just as likely that the philosophy had settled deep into his bones at the moment of his conception. Repaying debts, or in this case, a kindness, was just part of his makeup, as much a part of him as his dark blond hair or his deep blue eyes.

Adhering to his philosophy set Hank on his course of action the moment he hung up the telephone after vainly trying to find a way to express his gratitude to Fiona. Though he might talk slowly, his mind was lightning fast and he usually made it up quickly. This time was no exception. He was going to meet this shy Good Samaritan in person.

It wouldn't hurt to pick up a bouquet of flowers while he was at it, either, Hank decided.

Flipping through the same telephone directory

he'd used to locate Painless Parties, he looked for a florist that would be on his way there.

Hank found one approximately two blocks from his destination. He jotted the address down below the one he'd already copied, then stuffed the piece of paper into his shirt pocket as he hurried out the front door. It was Saturday and far too beautiful a day to waste inside, or by himself.

His car, a soothing metallic green import, sat waiting for him in the driveway. Unlike the house he now occupied, the sports car was his. A gift to himself after landing the largest advertising account in the history of Fraser and Smith, the firm he had outgrown and left behind in Butte, Montana.

As he turned the key, the car purred like a kitten being scratched in a particularly favorable place. He'd gotten it for a song from its previous owner because it had had myriad problems. A natural knack for car repair had enabled him to get it up and running quickly. That and his brothers and sister, all of whom insisted on donating some time and energy toward the sports car's recovery program.

He had the car; now he needed a house. He'd buy a home here soon enough, Hank promised himself, backing out. For now, he was renting, but once he got six months under his belt with his new firm, a house was going to be the first thing on his agenda. Though he was far from greedy, he felt a man needed to own certain things. The roof over his head was one of them.

That he was on the path toward getting it was due

to a melodic voice on his answering machine. A voice he was now determined to put a face to.

Whether the lady actually realized it or not, she was a lifesaver. If not for her, he would have missed making the best connection—so far—of his career. Collins Walker was a prestigious advertising firm that needed an experienced person to head up their newest division. He fit the bill perfectly and needed the opportunities that working for the large firm provided. They were made for each other.

But it would have been a match destined never to materialize if Ms. Fiona Reilly hadn't chosen to intervene at the right moment.

That kind of thing, he thought, pulling up in front of the florist, simply could not go unnoticed. If she didn't want to go out to dinner with him, he could accept that. But the least he could do was send her flowers.

Or bring them to her.

His mouth curved in response as the scent of flowers assailed him when he walked into the small shop. *Sure beat walking into a stable first thing in the morning,* he mused, thinking of the ranch he'd grown up on. He and his brothers and sister were raised on manners and hard work. That included pitching in and pitching hay before dawn was even a faint glimmer on the horizon.

Carnations, he decided after a beat, seeing them on display behind the glass casing. A profusion of carnations. He'd never met a woman yet who didn't like carnations. Not even his sister, Morgan, who, as the youngest, always tried to be as rough and tumble as the rest of them.

Yes, carnations. Just personal enough, yet not quite intimate.

Friendly.

Like him.

It was his mother who had taught him to give everything the personal touch. That meant calling instead of faxing, and in this case, bringing rather than sending.

It was an edict that Hank firmly believed had gotten him where he was today: way ahead of some of his contemporaries at Fraser and Smith who were admittedly more talented but lacked that certain something when it came to making presentations and dealing with clients.

Hank liked to call it heart.

If there was anything he had, he thought as he made his selection and waited for the saleswoman to ring it up, it was heart.

Ten minutes later, pleased with his choice and leaving a somewhat smitten woman in his wake, Hank walked out of the shop. With the greatest of care, he placed the flower arrangement on the passenger seat, then slowly folded himself up to fit in behind the wheel of his vehicle. Hank loved his sports car and knew it was great for his image, but he had to admit there were times it was hell on his legs and back. At a rangy six-four he'd become accustomed to not having things fit exactly right. This included his car.

Turning the engine on, he eased down on the accelerator and pulled away from the curb. He was a man with a mission.

No one answered.

Hank pressed the doorbell again, listening this time to see if the thing actually worked. His father had disconnected their doorbell once to see about making it ring louder. It had never worked after that. Not that they had had all that many visitors on the ranch. The Shady Lady was too out of the way for most people. While growing up, he'd been itchy to leave himself and move to the big city. The same was true of all his siblings, except for Kent, who'd been born clutching a saddle horn.

"Never thought I'd miss that old place," he murmured to himself as he pressed the doorbell again.

The doorbell worked, all right, but it was obviously being ignored since no one came to answer it. Hank glanced back at the driveway. There was a van standing there, with a huge logo comprised of caricatures partying wildly painted across its side. The van was backed up to the garage, its doors unlocked and partially open. He figured that meant someone was home.

After three more attempts. Hank was debating his next move when he heard a faint cry of distress coming through the open window next to the front door. There was definitely someone home. Maybe they just couldn't hear him ringing.

Curious, wondering if someone needed help, Hank

backed away from the door and began searching for another way in other than the open window. He didn't fancy getting shot. Maybe there was a back door that was accessible. Gamely, he began to circle the house, keeping one eye peeled for a dog. His mother hadn't raised any idiots.

Fiona groaned again. Feeling suddenly boneless, she sank down onto a stool by the counter. She couldn't have heard right. This had to be some kind of a bad dream.

"No, no, you can't do this to me, Alex, you just can't."

The male voice on the other end of the line sighed deeply into her ear. "I didn't exactly do it to *you,* Fiona. I did it to my ankle and believe me, spraining it wasn't exactly something I had penciled in on my list of things to do for today."

She knew what she'd said was unreasonable, but with a wedding reception for an "intimate gathering" of two-hundred guests to face she wasn't feeling all that reasonable.

"Now where am I supposed to get another waiter on such short notice?"

Alex's tone was bordering on impatience. Fiona strained to make out what he was saying above the din of background noise.

"Call the temp service. It's where you got me originally," he reminded her.

She'd thought of that as soon as Alex had told her he was calling from the hospital ER, but then discarded the idea. It would be physically impossible to get someone here on time. And besides, there were other complicating factors to consider. She felt as if she'd just stepped into a nightmare.

"It's where I got you with five days to spare," Fiona noted, nervously dragging her hand through a sea of reddish-brown hair. "Not five minutes. I wish you'd called sooner."

"Hey, I'm really sorry, Fiona." There was sympathy in every syllable. "My nephew's skateboard was just in the wrong place at the wrong time. Or maybe I was. When I went flying, I thought for sure I was going to land on my head."

"Then you would have cracked the cement, not sprained your ankle."

What the hell was she going to do? Fiona wondered. Her brain scurried like a high-powered mouse sniffing out the right corridor leading to the sliver of cheese. Right now, the cheese perversely insisted on eluding her.

"Very funny. Seriously, this is the first chance I've had to call you. I've been buried in this emergency room all morning."

He made her feel guilty. She was going on about a wedding reception while he was there, hurting.

"I'm sorry, I shouldn't be carrying on this way. There'll be other weddings." She hoped. "You just get better, I'll manage," she told him cheerfully. With a deep sigh, she replaced the receiver. "I'll just grow another pair of arms in the next half hour, that's all," Fiona muttered under her breath.

This was *really* going to be a problem. There was no way she and Bridgette would be able to manage on their own. Not with all those drinks to make and the buffet to manage. And there was no one she could call at this late hour.

Fiona closed her eyes, praying for a miracle. "Just a tiny, kitchen-size one. You'd hardly notice it was missing," she murmured to whatever patron saint had been assigned to fledgling caterers.

As if in response, Fiona heard Velcro suddenly screech, followed by a very male gasp. The next moment there was rather an urgent knock on her kitchen door.

Patron saints didn't knock. Even unnamed ones.

"Now what?"

Feeling hugely put upon and, for once in her life, not the least bit friendly, Fiona strode to her back door. From the sound of Velcro's screech, the cat had found someone new to stick her sharp little claws into. Fiona shook her head. Other people had pets, she had an attack cat.

She didn't have time for this.

Frazzled and without a decent solution to her problem, Fiona swung open the door.

"Yes?" she demanded just as she came face-to-bud with a rather large, fragrant arrangement of pink and white carnations.

"Is this cat yours?"

The question, coming from above the center of the bouquet, was laden with barely suppressed pain. A direct result of Velcro's claws, which had to be dig-

ging into the man's leg. All Fiona could think of was
two inches higher and the florist deliveryman would
have turned into a soprano.

Velcro meowed rather loudly, as if to negate whatever it was the man was saying.

Gingerly, trying not to seem as if she were being
too personal, Fiona detached Velcro's claws one by
one from the stranger's leg. When he sucked in his
breath, she winced in sympathy.

Holding Velcro to her, Fiona backed away.

"I'm so sorry," Fiona apologized. "Would it help
to know that she does that out of affection?"

Hank'd known a woman like that once. But luck-
ily, not for long. Balancing the bouquet, he quickly
rubbed his leg, surprised that there was no blood
spurting out. He could have sworn the cat had sunk
her claws in clear down to the bone.

"Affection, huh?" He brushed cat fur from his
pant leg. "I'd sure hate to run into your cat when
she's mad, then."

"Not a pretty sight," Fiona assured him, petting
Velcro as she stared at the stranger.

He, however, was. Pretty. Very pretty, in a sensual, bone-melting sort of way, Fiona decided. The
man's face, tanned from the sun, was comprised of
an incredible number of planes and angles that somehow formed a gentle, sensitive face, rather than a
hard one.

Fiona blinked, forcing herself to focus. This
wasn't the time to notice things like that. She had a
crisis on her hands, an attack cat *in* her hands and a

gorgeous arrangement of carnations practically in her face, not to mention a gorgeous man on her doorstep.

She nodded at the flowers, stroking Velcro a little harder than she should. "Are those for me?"

She looked exactly the way Hank had expected her to, he thought. Lively, sparkling. He'd been wrong about the hair, though. He'd thought she'd be a blonde. The smoky auburn hair was striking.

Hank presented the carnations to her. "Yes. I'm—"

"Tall," Fiona suddenly blurted. The man from the florist's was tall. Maybe even taller than Alex, she thought. Maybe there really *was* a patron saint for fledgling caterers.

"Well, yes, I am, but—" Hank had been this height since he was thirteen, waiting for everyone else to catch up. Not many had. Hank was accustomed to people pointing out the obvious.

Perfect, he was perfect. Fiona thought of the uniform that was hanging in her hall closet, the one Alex always wore whenever she used him on a catering assignment. This man looked as if the uniform had been made for him.

Like a tailor taking one final measurement, Fiona began to circle the stranger.

"Perfect," she pronounced again, this time out loud.

Hank had never had a woman sound quite this forward before. "Excuse me?"

Fiona hardly heard him. Her mind was humming. "Are you busy?" *Oh, please, don't let him be busy.*

"Right now, I mean—are you busy?" she repeated when he didn't say anything. The answer to her prayers looked a little stunned. "I mean, you don't have any other flowers to deliver, do you?"

Lost now, Hank had absolutely no idea what this woman with the wild, gypsy hair was getting at. "No," he responded cautiously.

A huge sigh of relief escaped her. "Wonderful. How would you like to make some money for about three hours' work?"

Maybe she wasn't as innocent as she looked. Hank's eyes narrowed as he studied her. He was usually a pretty good judge of character, but it seemed that he'd miscalculated this time.

"Just what is it you have in mind?"

Fiona's mind was racing, trying to cover all bases. What if he was clumsy? No, no one this good-looking could possibly be a klutz. There had to be some unwritten law about that.

"How's your balance?"

The only reason Hank's mouth didn't drop open was that it had frozen in place.

"Excuse me?" He was trying very hard not to let his imagination take over and run away with him, but it wasn't easy.

Fiona realized that her mind was going faster than her tongue. She tried to get control of herself. "Can you hold a tray?"

His eyes never left her face. "While doing what?"

"Serving." Quickly she set Velcro on the floor and took the man's elbow. Pulling hard, Fiona tugged him into the hallway. And into her dilemma. "The waiter I had lined up for the wedding I'm catering this afternoon just called to say he sprained his ankle. I'm in a real bind. I can't get anyone on such short notice, certainly not anyone as tall as he was—"

"Height matters?" Hank still couldn't make any sense of this. Just who was going to be at this wedding she was catering, a basketball team?

Fiona was getting ahead of herself again. No wonder he was having trouble keeping up. The man spoke as if he had all the time in the world to form words. She, however, did not. Fiona struggled to curb her impatience. She *needed* this man.

"It does if the only uniform you have hanging in your closet is made to fit a man who's six-four." She crossed her fingers as she opened the closet. "Are you six-four?"

Now it was beginning to come together for Hank. "And a quarter."

Fiona could have hugged him. "Bless you." She was already reaching into the closet. "You'd really be doing me a tremendous favor and the job pays fifty." Pulling the uniform out, she handed it to him.

Shifting the flowers he was still holding to one side, Hank took the hanger she thrust at him. "But I—"

She had no time to argue about money. "I can go as high as sixty." The look she gave him bordered on begging. At the moment, Fiona was far from proud. Just desperate. "Please."

If ever there was a surefire way to erase a debt,

this was it. Hank didn't even hesitate. "Sure." And then he remembered. He looked at the bouquet. "Don't you want these?"

"Oh, yes, sure." Hastily, she accepted the bouquet, then parted several of the flowers, looking for a card. She glanced at the person she took to be the deliveryman. "There's no card."

Since he'd had every intention of delivering the flowers in person, Hank had seen no reason to write one. "No, I—"

But she was way ahead of him again.

"Lost it, that's okay." He was bailing her out. The last thing in the world Fiona wanted was to make him think he'd done something wrong. "I've lost plenty of things myself."

She could always call the florist later to find out who'd sent the carnations. They were undoubtedly from a client. She wasn't in the habit of receiving flowers, but whenever she did, they were always from clients. These had probably come from the Albrights. The couple had been especially grateful for the job she had done for their twins.

Fiona saw that he looked unconvinced. "No reason to beat yourself up over losing it." One arm around the bouquet, the other around his arm, Fiona urged him back into the kitchen. "Believe me, you'll be more than making up for it by helping me out of this jam."

In what seemed to Hank like one fluid motion, she took down an empty jar that had, until this morning, held bow-tie pasta. She filled it with water and placed the carnations into it.

He could almost feel the charged energy bouncing around this woman.

"Does everyone around here talk as fast as you do?" he asked, wondering for the first time if he was going to be able to keep up in Southern California after all.

"No, only when they're having a crisis." She pointed him toward the bathroom. "Now please, put on the uniform. And hurry. I've got to be over there in half an hour." She glanced at her watch, although it was entirely unnecessary. Fiona had the time down pat. She could feel the minutes ticking away in her soul. "Bridgette's already at the house, setting up."

His hand on the doorknob, Hank paused. "Bridgette?"

Agitated, Fiona placed her hand over his and turned the knob, opening the door. "My sister."

Ever so slowly, he looked down at her hand, then back up at her. Suddenly aware of what she was doing, Fiona dropped her hand. A warm flush danced through her like summer fireflies fanning their wings against the sultry night.

"Is this her business?"

"No, it's mine." Her self-consciousness faded. Fiona flashed a grin, lighting up the entire kitchen. "Can't you tell?"

At the moment there wasn't a whole lot Hank could tell, except that he'd somehow managed to wander into the path of a twister and had gotten sucked up.

And he had to admit that it wasn't an altogether unpleasant experience. All he had to do was wait until his breath managed to catch up to him.

"Wait," she cried just as he was about to close the door behind him. "What do I call you?"

He often ran into that. Most people took one look at him and declared that he didn't look like any Henry they knew. "My friends call me Hank."

She nodded. "Hank." And then she smiled beguilingly. "Thank you."

"Sure thing."

Fiona hurried off to change the moment the bathroom door was closed. There wasn't much time left. Accustomed to wiggling into her uniform quickly, she was out just as the bathroom door opened again and her "kitchen-size miracle" emerged.

Yes, Virginia, there is a Santa Claus. She smiled, surveying the fit. "It looks terrific on you. Better than on Alex."

She especially liked the way the pants adhered to his muscular legs and butt. Maybe no one would notice if he did happen to be clumsy. At any rate, none of the women would.

She'd changed, as well, Hank noticed immediately. Changed into a uniform that was guaranteed to wander through many a man's fantasies. Certainly his. It was a maid's outfit, black, trimmed in white lace with a distractingly short skirt. And she was now wearing heels. Black heels that made her more than three inches taller.

He liked her at this height, he thought. Her face was closer to his. That made it rather nice.

Hank made no effort to suppress the smile blooming on his lips. "Does that outfit come with fishnet stockings?"

She looked down, as if to check. "No. Just Suntan," she said, giving him the name of the color stamped on the side of the panty hose box.

The grin definitely went with the drawl, Fiona decided. "Last time I saw legs that long and pretty, I fell in love."

Uh-oh, she thought, maybe this wasn't such a good idea after all.

"They belonged to the filly my father gave me," he continued. "Gwendolyn was my first love, and we were an inseparable pair. I was five."

Fiona let out the breath she was holding, feeling instantly at ease. "Your first love was a horse?"

"Yes, ma'am, except that Gwendolyn thought she was people."

She knew all about the way animals fancied themselves. "Velcro thinks she's an attack cat."

He laughed. The sound, deep, resonant and sensual, wound its way through her system, finally lodging itself in her gut.

"Yes, I already know that," he said.

"Sorry." She couldn't help laughing herself. Some of the tension that naturally accompanied her on these assignments seemed to fade into the background. But it didn't dim her awareness of the time—and the fact that it was growing short.

"I've got to get the rest of the food over there before the reception starts." She picked up one box of hors d'oeuvres she'd packed away and handed it to him, then picked up a second one herself. "The van's out front." Not waiting for a response, Fiona led the way.

Outside, she looked around, expecting to see another vehicle parked at the curb. Instead, there was an impressive-looking sports car she didn't recognize. The woman across the street undoubtedly had a new boyfriend. Ever since her divorce had become final—Fiona had catered her "divorce party"—the woman had been going through boyfriends as if they were tissues. This car probably belonged to the latest candidate.

"Where's your van?"

He looked at her, wondering where the question had come from. "I don't have a van."

Why wouldn't a deliveryman drive a van? Where did he put the flowers he delivered? "How did you get here?"

"In that." He pointed toward the sports car.

That was his? "Just how much do they pay you to deliver flowers?"

With every passing minute, Hank felt as if he were going deeper and deeper into the forest. "'They' don't pay—"

"You enough. Yes, I know." She placed the box she was holding onto a shelf in the back of the van, then took his. "A common feeling, I'm sure. That's how I felt, working for someone else. Underpaid, under-appreciated." She slammed the doors shut and secured them. "That's one of the reasons I began my own company." She flashed an unconscious smile, then headed for the front of the van. "That way, there's no one telling me what to do—at least, not for long."

He was wrong, Hank thought. She moved faster than his filly had. And the legs were definitely better. "Could they?"

Fiona turned around to look at him. "What do you mean?"

His eyes swept over her. She was small, compact, but then, so was dynamite. He wondered what it was like when she finally erupted. Would it be all noise, or would there be the kind of fireworks that lit up the sky on the Fourth of July? "I get the feeling that no one could tell you what to do if you didn't want to do it."

It took Fiona a moment to pull herself together. The look in his eyes was positively hypnotic. And she didn't want to go where his smile was taking her. It was much too warm and decadent there.

"That's one of the nicest things anyone has ever said to me."

"That, I find very hard to believe."

Despite her best efforts, his smile wound through her like warm, sultry sea breezes, seducing her. "You're very easy to talk to." So easy, she realized, that she hadn't even thought to introduce herself. "By the way, I'm Fiona Reilly."

"Yes, I know. And I'm—"

Of course he'd know. He was delivering the flowers to her. She was such a dummy at times.

"A godsend," Fiona concluded. She ducked into the vehicle, motioning him over to the passenger seat. "C'mon, get in the van, we're going to be late."

Feeling more amused than confused, Hank got in next to her. He recalled hearing that line, or a similar sentiment, uttered by the white rabbit as he ran down the rabbit hole. Except that this time, it was "Alice" who was dragging him down the rabbit hole in her wake.

He looked at Fiona as he put on his seat belt. "Are things always this hectic?"

"Only if I'm lucky." Fiona revved the engine, easing the van out of the driveway and praying that every light from here to the Kellermans' house was frozen in her favor. From the corner of her eye, she saw the strange look he was giving her. Probably thought she was crazy. He wouldn't be the first. "It's June, the month of weddings. And this year, the personal, homey touch is in. And if there's anything I can do, it's give things that homey touch." She turned the van as sharply as she dared. "Hang on, it's going to be a bumpy ride."

Hank had already surmised that.

3

―――――◄―――――

"Well, it's about time you got here. I know you're the boss, Fiona, and I'm only your sister pitching in but—"

Easily frazzled, Bridgette was apparently way beyond her frazzling point when Fiona approached. As Bridgette turned around to face her, her mouth dropped open, the rest of her tirade vanishing. The tray in her hands, loaded with empty glasses, tilted just enough to threaten to send everything on it sliding down to the patio.

Hank quickly elbowed Fiona aside and made a grab for the edge of the tray. Envisioning the mess created by the shattered glasses, Fiona tried to gather the glasses before they crashed ignobly at the same time.

Rushing, they bumped against each other, their hands tangling. The glasses were rescued and contact was made, leaving a definite impression on both.

Feeling self-conscious without fully understanding why, Fiona slowly withdrew her hands from the glasses, keeping them steady. That was more than she could say for her pulse.

"Nice save," Fiona congratulated him, mustering a half smile. She waited for her heartbeat to become at least partially regular. "I guess that answers my questions about your sense of balance."

He grinned, releasing his own hold on the tray. "Guess so."

Bridgette plopped the tray onto the table without so much as a glance. There was something far more important than rescuing a handful of glasses going on here.

She'd expected to see Alex walking in behind Fiona. Dependable, amiable, he still had the kind of face that made Abraham Lincoln good-looking by comparison. Seeing the sexy stranger instead had caught her completely off guard.

"Excuse me," she murmured to the man. Moving briskly, Bridgette commandeered Fiona's arm and tugged her over to the side.

Fiona opened her mouth to protest, but never got the chance to form any words. Bridgette talked fast when she wanted to.

"Where on *earth* did you find him?" Bridgette asked breathlessly.

Trust Bridgette to focus on a good-looking man instead of their reason for being here in the first place. "He found me, actually. That's the delivery-man from the florist. Hank."

Looking over Fiona's shoulder, Bridgette devoured Hank with her eyes, one tidy, delectable morsel at a time. He did things to a tuxedo she could only dream about.

"Well, he can certainly make a delivery to me any day." Beaming, she looked at her sister, a teacher seeing her backward pupil finally graduating. "Fiona, I'm proud of you, but isn't this rather a strange first date?"

Fiona uncoupled herself from Bridgette's grasp. There were hors d'oeuvres to heat and a five-tier wedding cake to put together. She didn't have time for this nonsense.

"Date?" she echoed incredulously. Where had her sister gotten that idea and why in heaven's name would she bring a date with her while she was working? "He's not my date, Bridgette," she said in a hoarse whisper, "he's the waiter."

That would have been the natural assumption, given the outfit he was wearing, but all Bridgette could think of was that the man looked stunning in basic black.

As an afterthought, she glanced around. "Where's Alex?"

Fiona hurried back to the van. Out of the corner of her eye, she saw the object of Bridgette's adulation following. At least he didn't have to constantly be instructed.

"In the emergency room, nursing a sprained ankle courtesy of his nephew. The deliveryman showed up just when I needed a miracle." Opening the back of the van, she raised her voice above a whisper. "He even fits perfectly into the uniform."

Bridgette slanted a sly glance at her before looking

over her shoulder at the man coming up behind them. "I wonder what else he fits perfectly into."

Hands filled with the hors d'oeuvres she had boxed, Fiona rolled her eyes. "Bridgette, you are oversexed."

Bridgette sighed as the man smiled at her before taking the box from Fiona. "There's no such thing." The statement was not uttered as quietly as it might have, given the topic. She adjusted her uniform, bringing her shoulders back and her best feature forward.

Fiona could only shake her head. She took out the bottom section of the wedding cake she'd made at five this morning, carefully easing the box from the shelf and keeping it steady. "Remind me to send a get well card to Brian."

Bridgette stretched out her hands, dutifully accepting the box. "Why? He isn't sick."

Two boxes piled on top of each other, Fiona led the way back to the garden. Her mouth curved as she glanced at her sister. "No, but if I know you, the poor man's probably suffering from exhaustion."

Bridgette smiled broadly. "Ha, you should be so lucky."

Entering the garden, Fiona looked at the man fate had placed on her doorstep at exactly the right moment. He'd put the box on the table and had opened it up and was now waiting for her.

"Yes, maybe I should," she murmured, more to herself than to Bridgette.

But Fiona knew better than that. Someone who

was as handsome as this man was probably married. And even if he wasn't, he could certainly have his pick of anyone. With his choices wide open, Fiona figured that didn't give her much of a chance. There was no point in even speculating about what might be because it wouldn't be. She had made her peace with things like that a long time ago.

"Let's get cracking," she announced to her team of two. She resisted the temptation to shake her sister. Bridgette looked as if she was about to start giggling like a schoolgirl at any second. "We haven't much time," she addressed Bridgette tersely. "The guests should be arriving very soon."

"What would you like me to do?" Hank asked, only to hear Bridgette's lusty laugh. He raised an eyebrow, waiting.

Suddenly the vamp, Bridgette replied, "You really don't want an answer to that."

Maybe she wouldn't shake her. Maybe she'd just hit her, Fiona thought, giving her older sister a black look that had absolutely no effect on her.

"You must be Bridgette," Hank said, smiling at her.

"I need help bringing the rest of the cake out," Fiona called out, going back to the van.

Bridgette waved a dismissive hand toward Fiona. Her eyes were riveted to eyes the color of a spring morning. "And you must be taken."

"Bridgette," Fiona called through gritted teeth, "we have work to do. This is no time to carry on an interview.'' Fiona shut her eyes, praying for strength. Why couldn't she have been an only child?

"Taken?" Hank wasn't sure what Bridgette meant. Did Fiona's whole family talk in circles?

Tuning Fiona out completely, Bridgette nodded as she drifted in the general direction of the driveway, her attention fastened to the man beside her. "Spoken for. Married. Involved.''

If it seemed like an invasion of privacy, he didn't appear to mind. "Nope, 'fraid not. None of the above.''

Fiona thrust a box into her sister's hands, then placed the larger one in his.

"Hurry,'' was all she said.

All she trusted herself to say. For now. Bridgette would get a dressing-down later, in private. Not that it would do any good. She was just grateful she was in too much of a rush to be properly mortified. That, too, would come later.

As Bridgette looked at her sister's back while the latter hurried to the garden, Bridgette thought she could hardly stand it. How could Fiona be so calm when the most gorgeous man either one of them had ever seen up close was occupying the same space as they were? And if that wasn't enough, he was unattached!

But that, Bridgette realized, was something Fiona probably didn't even know. Because Fiona wouldn't have asked. Bridgette's mind began to furiously conjure up plans that would bring the two of them together. Lucky thing for Fiona she wasn't an only child or she would probably succeed in working herself into an early grave—and arrive there alone.

All things considered, Fiona thought, in spite of the rather rocky beginning and Alex's no-show, the reception was going smoothly. They had caught a lucky break when the photographer had decided to detour to the local park on the way back from the church. He'd remained to take an entire roll of film of the happy couple and their entourage. It gave Fiona and company the breathing space they needed to finish setting up.

By the time the guests and wedding party arrived, the guinea hens were hot, the drinks cold and the wedding cake, freshly reassembled, was a work of art. Everything had turned out letter perfect, even to Mrs. Kellerman's critical eye.

Fiona kept an eye of her own on her protégé, worried that he might be overwhelmed by so many people.

She might have spared herself the worry.

Hank took to it like the proverbial duck to water. Water filled with women. Every time Fiona looked his way, he was surrounded by women, making requests or flirting shamelessly. She noticed more than one female guest slipping money into his breast pocket in exchange for a drink, or for clearing away an empty plate.

Or maybe the promise of something later, she thought suddenly.

This never happened when Alex worked with

them. But then, Alex's face was more inclined to stop a clock, not a heart.

"They're all over him," Bridgette rasped in her ear as she passed with another tray of guinea hens. She placed them on the table.

Fiona quickly arranged the hens on the serving platter. "Yes, I noticed."

Bridgette nudged her impatiently, as if this were a competition instead of an affair they were catering. "Well, get over there."

Fiona stared at her. Was Bridgette out of her mind? "And do what?"

Bridgette's eyes widened as if she was stunned Fiona had to ask. "Stake your claim."

Fiona emptied the tray, purposely not looking up. "The man is not a mountain."

"Hardly. Mountains aren't sexy." Bridgette took the tray from her, as if this was the only thing holding her back.

"You seem to forget that the man's a total stranger who's doing me a favor."

"Fine," Bridgette allowed, "let him do you an even bigger favor by not being a stranger any longer. The man is drop-dead gorgeous and single. They're swarming around him like piranhas in a feeding frenzy. *Do* something."

"I *am* doing something. I'm working." Fiona reclaimed the tray and marched back into the kitchen.

What in the world, Fiona fumed silently, was Bridgette thinking? This was neither the time nor the place to throw herself at the man. Actually, there never would be a time or place. Her self-confidence didn't run in that direction. Her father had seen to that. A tall, darkly handsome man, he'd been appalled by her plain appearance from the first and had never missed an opportunity to remind her of that. His pet name for her had been Plain Jane.

Years later, she'd learned that at one point he'd even accused his wife of infidelity because Fiona had been so plain while her parents and sister were all so striking. Looking back, her entire childhood had been marked by being the ugly duckling in a company of swans. By the time she became a swan herself, or so Bridgette said, it was too late to change her feelings of inadequacy.

"Damn it, girl," Fiona muttered under her breath, "stop hiding in the kitchen. You have work to do." She grasped a fresh tray of guinea hens and forced herself back to the reception.

The first thing she saw as she emerged was Mrs. Kellerman flirting with Hank. Mr. Kellerman was off to the side, quietly nursing a glass of wine, a mellow expression on his face.

Fiona and Mrs. Kellerman made eye contact and the woman drifted over to her, but not before caressing the hand of a man young enough to be her son.

"You did a fabulous job, my dear," Mrs. Kellerman declared. "I will definitely call about Janet's wedding in the fall. And I do hope you'll have the same young man helping you."

Fiona saw no reason to launch into explanations.

Instead, she did what she very seldom did. She lied. "Of course."

Mrs. Kellerman laughed. "Good. And before I forget, here." She stuffed an envelope into Fiona's pocket. "I'm sure you'll find everything in order." She glanced over her shoulder. The expression on her face was positively wistful. "And a little something extra besides."

"Here, let me help you with that."

Surprised, Fiona looked up from the garbage bag she was struggling with. Bridgette had left shortly after the guests had departed, citing a "family commitment," which was code for, "I don't clean my mess, why should I clean anyone else's?" The newlyweds had long since gone off on their honeymoon and Mr. and Mrs. Kellerman had retired. That left her to tend to cleanup.

Trying to hurry, Fiona had forgotten about the impromptu waiter. Somehow she'd just assumed that one of the women at the reception had made off with him, as if he were one of the centerpieces at the tables.

Not waiting for her answer, Hank took the bag from her and hefted it with ease.

He certainly was a lot more helpful than Alex was, Fiona thought. She wondered if Hank might be willing to do this again, if conditions were right.

"Thanks." Taking out another plastic garbage bag, she shook it open and gathered the remainder of the trash. "And thanks for staying to help. I hate cleanup," she confided.

Hank thought of mucking the stables and laughed. The lady had no idea what real cleanup meant.

"We've got that in common." He brought the filled bag over to the side of the house where the rest of the trash was stored. Placing it beside the cans, Hank returned to see what else he could do. "I always tried to duck out of doing it as a kid."

Fiona tried to imagine what he had looked like as a kid. He probably had little girls volunteering to do his homework all through grade school.

"No, I mean I hate it because it means the party's over." She paused, reflecting as she looked around the garden.

It looked forlorn, but it was more than just the twilight creeping in. It seemed lonelier somehow. There had been tables and chairs laid out along the manicured lawn with balloons in the shape of doves and streamers hanging overhead. Half had been taken by the departing guests for their children. The rest hung limply, waiting to be discarded, their usefulness over.

Fiona brought a step stool over to a cluster of balloons closest to the house and climbed up. "There's something very sad about that. Take this wedding." Tugging, she pulled the streamers free. She handed them down to him, then reached for the balloons. "They've been planning it for months. I've got a mountain of faxes from the Kellermans, detailing everything from the kind of napkins to the frosting on the cake—in a combination of seven different ways.''

Hank held the step stool steady for her. He had to admit the view was inspiring. Her legs were gorgeous, withstanding scrutiny even at this proximity.

"I'm surprised you're not glad it's over, then.''

"Well, I am in a way.'' Fiona stretched to get the cluster that hung just out of reach. She certainly wouldn't miss dealing with Mrs. Kellerman's multiple phone calls. ''The headache part of it is over. But it still seems rather sad.'' Holding her breath, she stood on her toes and made a grab for another cluster of streamers. ''Months and months of preparation and then it's all over in just a few hours.''

Her thigh brushed against his cheek as he leaned forward to steady her. The stool tottered slightly. Hank felt a very strong sexual pull. He tried to keep his mind on the conversation. The lady was a little too unwittingly tempting for her own good.

"A lot of life's like that,'' he told her. ''But there's always something new to look forward to.''

"I guess you're right.'' Fiona laughed softly to herself. The next moment, she gasped as she pitched forward.

Hank knocked the falling stool out of the way with his leg as he quickly caught her. His hands were around her waist and he pulled her to him.

Heart hammering, Fiona looked down at Hank as she rested her hands on his shoulders. She felt like a dancer frozen in the air. ''That's the second nice save you made today.'' He smiled up at her, raising her body temperature by several degrees.

"Funny, I was just thinking it was my first."

"The glasses," she reminded him. It amazed her that she could sound so calm when her heart was speeding like a freight train down an incline.

"Oh, yeah. I forgot about them." His breath seemed to waft up to her, accelerating her heart rate to the point that she thought it would vibrate straight out of her chest.

"You can put me down now," she told him after a beat. Was it her imagination, or did she sound reluctant when she said that?

"All right."

Very slowly, he lowered her until her feet touched the ground. Her body brushed against his. The contact was minimal, a breeze touching flower petals as it moved along a meadow. The effect was a great deal stronger. Fiona felt as if she'd fallen victim to an electrical storm that assaulted her body from every angle, making it tingle and light up like a star.

She pressed her lips together just to keep from moaning.

"Maybe I should take down the rest of the decorations," Hank suggested.

"Maybe," she murmured. How long before she stopped tingling? He'd hardly touched her, for heaven's sake.

Switching positions, Fiona found herself looking up at a very muscular set of glutei maximi. The man had a very nice butt, she thought. The next minute she realized that he had been privy to pretty much the same view, except that she hadn't been wearing pants. Color crept up her face.

Handing down the next cluster of decorations, Hank looked at her when she didn't take them. Fiona was staring at her feet. He had a hunch he knew why and the reason tickled him. His mother, he thought, would have loved this woman instantly.

So would his brothers, but for an entirely different reason.

Clearing his throat to catch her attention, Hank handed her the balloons when she looked up.

Fiona could tell she amused him, and why not? Despite the soft pattern of speech and manners, he was undoubtedly accustomed to the company of sophisticated women. A club she didn't belong to.

Fiona forced her mind back on business. "I've got another wedding to cater next week," she began, feeling her way into the subject.

"You must be doing well." Effortlessly, he reached for another cluster of decorations and took the streamers down.

"Better than I used to," she allowed. Fiona nibbled on her lower lip. "Would you be interested in doing this again?"

Hank got down, then moved the step stool to a new location. "If you're in a bind."

It wasn't a bind exactly. She craned her neck, looking up. "With Alex out of commission, I'd have to hire another temporary waiter. Since you worked out so well…" Maybe that wasn't worded correctly.

"I mean, you seem to have a flair for this," she continued quickly, "and if it doesn't cut into your job with the florist—"

Hank's eyebrows drew together as he tried to follow. "My job with the florist?"

"Yes, delivering flowers."

Hank came down the step stool slowly, his eyes on hers. Where had she come up with that notion? "I don't deliver flowers."

Fiona was completely lost. Why was he looking at her as if she was spouting gibberish? "But you delivered mine—"

"Yes, because I wanted to bring them in person." Instinctively, Hank took her hand in his to keep her in place. She had the look of a deer about to bolt out of the clearing and into the forest.

"I don't under—"

And then it hit him. Fiona didn't know who he was. "I'm Hank Cutler. The wayward fax," he added, hoping to jar her memory when she continued staring at him mutely.

Embarrassment washed over Fiona, a tidal wave this time, threatening to drown her. He had to think she was a certifiable cretin. "Oh, no, I've made a terrible mistake."

Hank grinned in response. It was the kind of grin that was pure boyish and all man at the same time. She felt her stomach muscles tightening even as she stood there wishing that the ground would open up and put an end to her misery.

"Not so terrible," he assured her, his voice soft,

almost lazy, as it left his mouth. "I've been mistaken for worse things than a deliveryman. Oh, by the way, I believe this is yours."

Hank began emptying his pocket of all the bills that had been pressed on him during the reception. It turned out to be rather a large wad.

She hadn't realized he'd collected that much. "Those are tips," she told him. "Traditionally, they belong to the waiter."

Honesty was a very sexy quality in the right woman, Hank thought. She was beginning to intrigue him on a completely different level.

"But I'm not a waiter," he reminded her. "Since you're the one who was doing the catering, I figure any resulting gratuities belong to you." When she still didn't reach for the money, Hank took her hand and pressed the bills into her palm. His eyes on hers, he closed her fingers around the wad.

The exchange of money had never felt quite so sexy to her before.

Fiona blinked. Her brain kept throbbing "idiot" over and over again like a flashing neon sign. She hadn't even asked his full name, just pressed him into service. Anyone with half a brain would have asked for that information. If she had, then she would have known who he was and she wouldn't have made such a fool of herself.

Fiona had to know. "Why did you come over?"

He cocked his head, as if trying to divine what she was getting at. "You drove me, remember?"

Fiona shook her head. "No, I mean to my house.

Why did you come?'' Why would someone who was so handsome take the time to come looking for a woman?

Hank shrugged. He was unaccustomed to explaining his actions. ''You wouldn't let me take you out to dinner and I wanted to find some way to say thanks. My sister likes carnations, so I thought maybe I should send some. But that seemed pretty impersonal, so I brought them instead.'' He grinned again. ''You did the rest.''

Yes, Fiona certainly did. Self-conscious, she shifted beneath Hank's gaze. ''You could have told me who you were.''

''I said my name was Hank,'' he noted.

''It says Henry on the résumé,'' she protested.

''Henry's more formal.'' He smiled into her eyes. ''We weren't being formal.''

There was something in her eyes—distress, Hank thought—that reached out to him. Slowly, he slid the tips of his fingers along her cheek, then watched, fascinated, as her pupils seemed to grow larger.

''And you say 'please' with more heart and conviction than anyone I've ever met.'' With a half shrug, he slid his hands into his back pockets. ''Besides, this was rather fun.''

Bridgette always griped that it was nothing but hard work. And Alex frequently complained that there was too much to do. Fiona had thought that there was something wrong with her for feeling that all this was an enjoyable madness. That Hank voiced a similar sentiment caught her off guard.

"It was?"

"Yeah. I don't do this for a living," he reminded her. "It's always fun when it doesn't count."

Was that his philosophy when it came to relationships and women, as well?

Of course it was, Fiona thought, annoyed with herself for even wondering. He wasn't married, was he? Women flocked to him like the last glass of water at an oasis in the Sahara, didn't they? Fun was probably all that counted with someone like Hank Cutler and she couldn't fault him in the least.

Needing something to do with her hands, Fiona began popping the balloons so they could be disposed of. "Still, you probably think I'm an idiot."

She was doing that with a vengeance, Hank thought, watching her jab the pin into one balloon after another. "No, I think you're a very driven, very energetic lady." His eyes became positively wicked as he added, "And I still think that outfit would look better with fishnet stockings."

Hank had the pleasure of watching a light pink hue climb up along the cheek he'd just brushed his fingers against. He hadn't thought women blushed anymore. And he certainly hadn't thought that seeing a woman blush would affect him in any manner.

Hank guessed he was wrong on both counts.

"I'll keep that in mind," Fiona murmured. Finished, she went to pick up her purse from where she had left it. Fiona counted out sixty dollars and held it out to Hank.

"What's this?" he asked.

"Your salary. You earned it." When he made no move to take it, she added, "We agreed on sixty."

"I didn't agree." He wasn't about to take her money. "Keep it. Consider it a favor."

She considered that. And the consequences. "That would make me in your debt."

They seemed to think the same. Hank's laugh was low, surrounding her like a slow-moving fog coming in from the sea to hug the coast.

"I guess it would."

Fiona raised her chin. "I don't like being in debt."

They really did think alike about some things. The thought pleased Hank. He inclined his head. "We'll work something out. There is something you can do for me right now, though."

Fiona could have sworn her heart stopped beating for a split second. "What?"

Hank had the urge to kiss her then, but the common sense to know that the timing was clearly off. "Drive me back to my car."

The breath returned to Fiona's lungs. "Oh. Right. Sure." For a second she had thought he was going to kiss her. She was being stupid again, Fiona upbraided herself. "Let's go."

Struggling with something that felt very much like disappointment, Fiona gestured toward her van.

She was unusually quiet as she drove them back to her house, Hank thought. Not that he knew what her usual habit was, but he surmised from the small peek he'd had of her world before she realized who he was, that Fiona didn't remain quiet for very long no matter what was going on. He rather liked the sound of her voice.

"How long have you been doing this?"

Fiona had been so lost in thought, the question startled her. "Doing what?"

"Catering."

"Oh." She did a quick calculation. "About four years." Then, because he seemed interested, she added, "It started with a few parties for friends who hated to cook and then mushroomed to this when people kept asking my friends for their recipes."

"Is business good?" he asked.

Because it was ingrained in her from an early age that nothing she ever did was good enough, Fiona shrugged. "Yes, for now," she qualified. She'd been in it long enough to know that catering had its ups and downs.

"Do you advertise?"

She couldn't really call it advertising. "In the phone book." It was a tiny ad, but it was an ad. "Word of mouth takes care of me," she added when she saw the dubious look on his face.

Hank was the first to agree that word of mouth was a powerful tool, but in this day and age, it was not enough. Not if she wanted to be a success, and he had a strong hunch that she did. "An ad campaign would go a long way in taking better care of you."

"That takes money."

Hank began to see how he could really pay her back. "Most of the time."

The look he gave her as he said it curled her toes so tightly, Fiona could feel the tips of her hair turning into springs.

4

Fiona pulled up the hand brake as she parked the van in her driveway. Advertising was always an expensive proposition. She turned to look at him. Just what was it that Hank was suggesting?

"I don't think I understand."

There was a tiny furrow between her eyebrows. Hank resisted the temptation of smoothing it with his fingertip just to see if he could.

"Why don't we go grab a cup of coffee somewhere and I'll tell you what I had in mind?" he proposed amiably.

He had a feeling that she might appreciate being served for a change instead of doing the serving. Besides, he rather liked the idea of being alone with her. There was something about her, about the nervous energy that seemed to surround her, that intrigued him.

The moment the thought of the two of them sitting opposite each other in a one-on-one situation registered, Fiona ceased being the owner of a catering business and reverted to being the gangly daughter in the family portrait. Even though she hated the self-image, hated the fact that she labored under its influence, she couldn't break the hold it had on her.

Fiona shrugged, looking past his head into the darkness. Though she tried to ignore it, she could feel her pulse jumping. *Idiot.* "I'm really rather tired tonight."

She'd probably been up early this morning, preparing everything for the reception, Hank thought. He'd already seen how thorough she was. He didn't blame her for being exhausted. Disappointed, Hank withdrew the invitation.

"Sure. I understand." He shifted beneath the seat belt, reaching into his pocket for his wallet. "Here." Opening the wallet, he removed a business card and held it out to her. "Why don't you take this and give me a call when you're ready to discuss the possibilities?"

Possibilities. The possibilities that were occurring to Fiona right now had nothing to do with dressing a guinea hen and everything to do with slowly undressing the man sitting in her passenger seat.

Surprised, Fiona caught herself. This was all Bridgette's fault. Her sister was definitely having a very bad effect on her.

"Um, there's your car." She gestured toward it needlessly. "And thanks again."

With effort, she purposely kept her voice cheerful and breezy as she got out of the van. Normally she'd unpack what was in it, no matter how tired she was. But she decided that the things could wait until after Hank had left. She didn't want him volunteering to help her. The sooner he was gone, the faster her head would clear.

But he didn't seem to be inclined to leave, despite her broad hint. Having gotten out on his side, Hank was standing in front of her house, obviously waiting for her. Partially bathed in shadow, Hank Cutler made an incredibly romantic figure. Fiona's heart fluttered a little just to look at him.

Searching for the key that fit the front door, she dropped the ring on the ground. Hank folded his lanky form with amazing ease as he bent for the keys, reaching them before she could. They bumped heads as he was on the way up and she on the way down. It jarred her, but he was still fast enough to steady her.

This was the second time he'd held her tonight, she thought. She could only wish that one of those times hadn't been by accident.

"Sorry," he apologized, releasing her. "I believe these are yours." He handed her the key ring.

"Thanks." Nervous, she rubbed her forehead where they'd made contact. "Is...is anything wrong?"

His eyes narrowed as he appeared to study her. "I don't think so."

There was no polite way to phrase this. "Then why aren't you leaving?"

His grin wound into her like a very sharp, very fast corkscrew. "Because you have my clothes."

Fiona closed her eyes. Of course she did. For a second she'd thought he was trying to get himself invited in. Stupid. She couldn't be behaving more like a village idiot than if she'd rehearsed the part for an entire week. "I forgot."

"I had a hunch." Hank watched her fumble with her keys, still trying to find the one that opened her front door. "This is just a shot in the dark, but am I making you nervous?"

"No, of course not."

Fiona pressed her lips together. She'd never been able to lie very well. In a way, it was an asset. People sensed that about her and knew they were dealing with someone they could believe. Someone honest. Right now, though, she wished she could lie like a con artist. Or at least feel as confident as one.

"Well," Fiona finally relented, holding her thumb and forefinger apart and forming a tiny space, "maybe just a little."

Fascinated, Hank leaned his shoulder against the doorjamb as she continued to look at keys and discard them on the ring. Just how many keys did this woman have?

"Why?" She'd aroused his curiosity. "I'm harmless enough."

Finding the right key, Fiona inserted it into the lock and turned the doorknob quickly. She flipped the lights on as she entered—every light between the doorway and the hall closet. There was something far too sensual about him as it was; she didn't need the darkness abetting him.

Fiona spoke before she thought. "Not with a smile like that you're not."

The answer tickled him. "Why, Fiona, I do believe you're flirting with me."

Horrified, her eyes widened in surprise at her own blunder.

"No, I'm not. I mean—" Fiona stopped herself. She knew that the more she talked, the worse this was going to get. Yanking the hanger out of the closet, she thrust it at him. "Here are your clothes."

He glanced at them. "Yup, they're mine, all right." He accepted the hanger, his eyes sweeping over her so slowly she could have sworn she was being touched. "It'll take me just a minute to change. You feel free to stay in that. I kinda like it on you." He closed the bathroom door behind him.

Fiona silently swore at herself. She'd forgotten she was still wearing the uniform. But if she ran upstairs to change now, he might take that as an indication that she wanted him to stay. The old "slipping into something comfortable" invitation.

He might take her remaining in the uniform the same way, she realized, torn. Damned if she did, damned if she didn't.

Story of her life, Fiona thought in mounting agitation. A sea of decisions to make and she could never be sure which one was the right one. Just which was the safe one.

In this case, neither was the safe one.

Before she could make up her mind, the door to the bathroom opened again. She looked at him in surprise. That had been awfully fast.

He read her expression correctly. "I was ten before we had a second bathroom put in. With all those people in the house wanting to use the facilities, you either learn how to get dressed fast or develop a very tough skin about being unceremoniously embarrassed.''

''So you learned how to dress fast.''

''Both, actually,'' he corrected. He handed Fiona the tuxedo, then rotated his shoulders, a panther stretching as he stepped out of sleep. ''There, that's better.'' He eyed the tuxedo. ''My dad used to call that a monkey suit. I'm beginning to understand what he meant.''

He was standing much too close to her, she realized. Trying hard not to trip over herself, Fiona stepped toward the closet and hung up the tuxedo. She searched for something neutral to say. ''Your dad, he's still in Montana?''

Nostalgia raised its head the way it did whenever he thought of his family and a place that would always be home to him no matter where he traveled and how old he became.

Following her into the hall, Hank laughed softly at her question. She looked at him quizzically.

''Yes, he's still in Montana. Couldn't get him out of there with anything short of dynamite. Maybe not even then. I told Dad I wanted the family to come down as soon as I got settled in. You know, look around, see what it was like here. Have a real reunion. But he said since there was only one of me, I could bring my tail up there instead of making everybody come down to see me.''

"Everybody?" Fiona echoed, interested despite her best efforts to keep this impersonal. His eyes seemed to shine when he spoke about his family. How did that feel? To have the good memories outweigh the bad? "How many people in an 'everybody'?"

He hooked his thumbs on the belt loops of his jeans and answered without skipping a beat. "Seven, but they're kind of scattered around now." He appeared to reconsider that. "Well, not Kent and my folks, of course, they're still living on the Shady Lady. But Quint, Will and Morgan all struck out on their own as soon as they could leave the ranch, moving so fast you could see the smoke coming from their feet for miles."

She had an image of three men, carbon copies of Hank, all rushing away from a small, weather-beaten ranch, and it made her smile. "Quint, Will and Morgan are your brothers?"

"Quint and Will are. But not Morgan." She didn't understand why he looked so amused until he added, "Morgan's my sister."

Maybe she would just have her foot sugar-coated and be done with it. That way, every time she stuck it in her mouth at least it would taste good. "Sorry."

Hank wondered why she felt so compelled to keep apologizing.

"No reason to be. Natural enough mistake with a name like that. Morgan's the youngest and my grandfather had gotten on my mother's case that none of the kids were named after him. When Morgan came along, he said he didn't care that she was a girl. He figured the name might bring her luck.''

Hank laughed, remembering Morgan's hot temper. A temper that hadn't gotten all that tamed, really. It just came in a prettier package these days. He pitied the man who'd try to tame her.

''Wasn't all that long ago that she *wanted* to be my brother. She always felt as if she had something to prove. No one would have ever accused her of being all sugar and spice back then. Even now, Morgan likes to think she's as tough as the rest of us.''

''Funny thing is, she is.'' Hank winked at Fiona.

The small flutter of lashes and skin went directly to her belly like brandy to an empty stomach. She had no buffer to shield her from it, or from the sexy smile that lifted the corners of a mouth created for the sole purpose of seduction.

''I'm glad you decided to stay in that,'' he added.

She lifted a shoulder, then let it drop quickly when she realized how helpless it made her seem. He'd just been talking about how strong his sister was, and here she stood, acting like one of the mice in *Cinderella,* scattering in the wake of the cat.

Except that the cat had never been this damn sexy.

''It wasn't a decision,'' she admitted. ''There wasn't enough time to change.''

They weren't going anywhere. She was all but escorting him out the door. Why was she worried about time? ''I'm afraid I don't follow. Why wasn't there enough time?''

This was just getting worse and worse. "Well, you were changing and..."

Hank put it together quickly. "You thought that I'd come looking for you if you weren't at the door when I opened it? Maybe walk into your room while you were still half dressed?"

He could see by the expression in her eyes that he'd guessed correctly and couldn't resist teasing her. He'd never in his life even come remotely close to forcing himself on a woman. It was against everything he believed in. But because he thought of himself as laid-back, he chose to let it amuse him rather than anger him.

"Maybe even crowd you a little, like this?" Hank maneuvered her until the wall was at her back and there was nowhere to go.

"No. Yes." Trapped and feeling frustrated by her reaction, Fiona was suddenly filled with exasperation. "Stop it."

Hank took a step back, though he had to admit that the close proximity was tantalizing. There was a fragrance in her hair—wildflowers, he thought—that was proving to be very arousing.

He didn't mean to laugh, but the expression on her face gave him no choice. When her eyes narrowed with annoyance, he held up his hand to ward off the tiny arrows her eyes were firing.

"Fiona, you are a pure delight." He thought of the last conversation he'd had with his mother before he'd boarded the plane. "You're nothing like the women my mother was worried I'd run into."

"Your mother was worried about *you?*"

The laughter faded in his throat, replaced by something else. A feeling, a tenderness entering where it had never existed before. Hank cupped her cheek with his hand. "Sure. Everyone knows that California girls are heartbreakers."

Her words came out slowly, like tiny beads being strung one at a time to form a necklace. Her eyes were mesmerized by his, unable to draw away.

"Then she'd be very happy you were here with me. I've never broken a heart in my life."

His mother wouldn't be the only one who was happy about logistics, he thought.

"Are you sure about that, Fiona?" Hank lowered his mouth until it was less than a breath away from hers. "Are you very sure about that?"

Fiona felt as if she were suffocating. There was no air left in her lungs. Why that should be such a pleasant sensation was beyond her. Maybe she was just getting too light-headed to think clearly.

"Positive," she whispered, afraid of waking herself up because it had to be a dream.

Her breath, sweet and enticing, drew him in, erasing the last stitch of space between them. Very softly, he touched his lips to hers.

All he wanted was a tiny sample, nothing more. Just one tiny sample.

But what he got, what he discovered, compelled him to deepen the kiss a little further. Greed, born in the wake of surprise, lifted its head, wanting more. Desiring more. The spark within his veins struck excitement, causing it to burn brightly as he savored the flavor of her lips.

His hand left her cheek and cupped the back of her head; his mouth pressed harder on hers. He was afraid of bruising her. And afraid of retreating.

The kiss seemed to deepen all on its own. He wasn't in charge anymore. At least not completely. Adventurous by nature, Hank felt just a pinprick of uncertainty as he felt himself being taken away. All he could think as he tightened his arms around her was that the last time his head had felt this way, he'd been kicked by a mule. He'd come to in a hospital bed.

This was infinitely more preferable.

Fiona forgot to be afraid. Forgot to draw back. Instead, confronted with such sheer maleness, she gave up all resistance and felt herself swept into the heart of the crackling inferno that blazed before her.

So this is what they meant by instant attraction.

As she wrapped her arms around his neck, Fiona's head fell back as the kiss overpowered her. There was no struggle on her part and no desire to put one up. All she wanted was to have this go on for a century or so. So she could make up for lost time.

Shaken, not quite sure exactly what to make of all this, Hank pulled his head back and looked down at this stick of dynamite he'd just handled. Talk about looks being deceiving.

He blew out a breath very slowly, silently waiting for his pulse to unscramble and do something about the meltdown in his brain.

The inexplicable feelings of tenderness were still there, hanging tenaciously like survivors of a shipwreck on to driftwood.

Unable to help himself, Hank lightly skimmed his fingers through her hair. "Don't be so positive, Fiona. Unless I miss my guess, there's a whole battalion of broken hearts in your wake."

Fiona blinked. The euphoria fell away like so much dead skin from a snake. What had been so beautiful a moment ago had turned ugly on her.

He was laughing at her, she thought, her back stiffening. The kiss had probably been a joke, as well. Turning, she pulled open the door. "It's late. Maybe you'd better go."

Hank stared at her uncomprehendingly. "Was it something I said?" The sweet, unassumingly sexy woman he'd kissed only a moment ago was gone, vanished like a magician's assistant in a magic act, to be replaced by a tiger.

Fiona wasn't about to give him the satisfaction of saying yes.

"No, but I have to get an early start tomorrow." Catching him off guard, she planted the heel of her hand on his chest and pushed him over the threshold. "Thank you for everything. Good night."

Before he knew what was happening, Hank found himself staring at the door instead of Fiona. What the hell had happened here? One moment he thought they were on their way to an incredible night of lovemaking; the next moment he was communing with a newly varnished door.

Mystified, shaking his head, Hank slowly walked away. Maybe his mother had the right idea about California girls. At the very least, they were a little crazy.

"You threw him out?"

Bridgette stared at her sister the following Monday as if her hair had suddenly turned into an array of hissing snakes. Too stunned to stand, she sank down at the long table Fiona had slavishly made at an adult education course in the local high school.

"Fiona, I thought insanity stopped in our family with Dad." She couldn't make herself believe it. Even Fiona wouldn't throw away a perfectly good man unused. "A gorgeous man and you threw him out?"

Fiona thumbed through her worn recipe book, looking for something exciting she could whip up as a sample to bring to Mr. and Mrs. Goldberg. It wasn't every day that a couple got to plan a celebration for their golden wedding anniversary. The last thing she wanted was to discuss the fiasco in her hallway the other night.

"I didn't throw him out," she said tersely. She placed a colorful Post-it note on page 543 to mark her place, then continued thumbing through the worn pages.

"Giving him the bum's rush is throwing in my book. Just what happened?"

Fiona shut the cookbook. All right, if Bridgette

wanted the truth, she'd give it to her. "He made fun of me."

Bridgette shook her head uncomprehendingly. "By kissing you?"

Restless, unable to find any peace for herself since Saturday night, Fiona got up and moved around the kitchen. There was nothing to clean, nothing to put in its proper place. She'd already done that. She settled for fussing with the spice rack.

"It wasn't the kiss, it was what he said." She shot Bridgette an accusing look over her shoulder, knowing exactly what her sister was thinking. That she was an idiot. "You wouldn't understand. You've been beautiful all your life."

That still explained nothing. "Thanks, but what does that have to do with anything?"

Fiona struggled to make her understand. "When we were growing up, whenever someone gave you a compliment, you knew they were telling you the truth. When I heard one, it was always from someone just being sarcastic."

Bridgette knew what Fiona had gone through. It was to her everlasting shame that she'd been too vain and taken with herself to intervene then. But there was no undoing the past. All she could do was try to make the present work for her sister.

Bridgette slipped an arm around Fiona's shoulders. "Look, kids say a lot of hurtful things. They find the one thing that bugs someone and tease the hell out of her." She looked into Fiona's eyes. "That doesn't mean it's true."

Fiona pulled away. She knew Bridgette was just trying to be kind. Their relationship had improved a thousandfold since they'd grown up. But that still didn't change the way things were.

She tried to act as if it didn't matter. That it was only a fact of life she'd accepted. But at the bottom, it still bothered her and it always would. "Dad said it was true. The mirror said it was true."

"Have you looked in that mirror lately?" Bridgette asked softly.

Fiona shrugged. It was all unimportant now. Only when someone like Hank came along was she reminded of the past and all the insecurities that had haunted her. "All right, so it doesn't crack anymore when I walk by, but someone like Hank is accustomed to the best. You saw the way women were swarming around him."

They might have swarmed, but Fiona was the one he'd kissed. "Your point being?"

Did she have to spell it out? "If he can have the very best, why would he be interested in me except to amuse himself?"

Bridgette had a feeling that Fiona had it all wrong, but she knew how stubborn she could be. "There's nothing wrong with amusement."

Fiona turned away from her and headed back to the table. Doggedly, Bridgette followed. "Sometimes it grows into something else. Besides, it's as good a place to start as any in forming a relationship."

"The only relationship I intend to have is with my business," Fiona reminded her, as if she hadn't already said the same thing a hundred times. But Hank had done one thing for her. He'd put the bug in her ear about advertising. It was now another goal to be met. "Maybe after a few more affairs like the Kellerman wedding, I'll have enough in the slush fund to consider an advertising campaign."

Bridgette's ears perked up. "What did you say Cutler did for a living?"

Fiona knew that look all too well. Bridgette was off and running again. She should have just lied and said that nothing had happened between her and Hank.

"Down, Bridgette. If and when I decide to fund an advertising campaign, it won't be with Hank's firm."

"And why not? You'll know you're getting your money's worth then."

Sometimes Bridgette's reasoning astounded her. "And why is that?"

Bridgette's expression could be termed nothing short of dreamy as she envisioned the man. "He's got honest eyes."

"Ha! Every time I saw you, you were looking at his butt, not his eyes."

Bridgette remained undaunted. "So he's got an honest butt, too. It's a set." As Fiona turned away, Bridgette placed her hand on her arm, stopping her. If only Fiona had learned how to tune out hurtful words as easily as she could tune out helpful ones. "Fiona, don't be foolish. This is perfect."

"For what?" she wanted to know. "For the business, or for me?"

Bridgette didn't even try to lie. Fiona would see right through it. "Both. From what I've seen, you *are* the business."

Maybe, but there was a simple little obstacle that couldn't be overlooked. "You forget, I don't have the money right now."

"Talk to the man," Bridgette implored. "I'm sure arrangements can be made. Maybe you don't have to fund everything up front."

"I don't get into deals asking for favors."

"Didn't he say that he owed you one, for alerting him that he'd sent his fax to you by mistake?"

Fiona shook her head. "We're squared away after Saturday. If anyone owes anyone, I owe him. He wouldn't take any money."

Bridgette's mouth dropped open. "You offered him money for kissing you?"

"No, for waitering." Fiona sighed in exasperation. "Bridgette, if you're going to pump me for information, at least pay attention when I give it to you."

But as far as Bridgette was concerned, she was paying attention. Very strict attention. To what she needed to hear.

5

"Let me get this straight."

Hank leaned forward in his chair and pulled over one of the many yellow pads he liked to keep handy in case an idea struck him. Though he considered himself on the cutting edge of technology, he had to admit that there was still nothing like the feel of pen to paper when it came to initial creativity.

Right now, he wasn't feeling all that creative, just bemused. He'd doodled a question mark on it when he'd first taken the call and discovered that Bridgette was on the other end. After listening to the woman talk nonstop for several minutes, the question mark was no closer to being erased than it had been to begin with.

He repeated what he'd gleaned from her ramblings. "You and your sister would like to arrange a meeting with me to discuss an advertising campaign for her catering business?"

There was a note of impatience in Bridgette's voice that she tried vainly to conceal. "That's what I've been saying for the last five minutes."

Hank knew a setup when he smelled one. "Fiona

didn't indicate any interest in advertising when I spoke with her about it." Unless showing him the outside of her front door somehow translated into being interested.

"She's had time to think about it and she's changed her mind. About everything," Bridgette added significantly, hoping that the blanket statement would cover anything that might need covering.

Though she'd pulled the story out of her sister bit by bit, Bridgette had no idea if there were any missing pieces that Fiona had failed to elaborate on. The tall, sexy stranger had seemed interested enough to her when she'd seen the two of them together. Maybe this would rekindle any fires that Fiona had doused.

"I see." As he spoke, the doodle turned into a stick figure of a woman balancing a huge wedding cake on a tray as she hurried to a waiting van. He gave the stick figure very curly hair that reached almost to her waist. And black high heels. "If she's so interested, why isn't she calling me herself?"

"She's busy today, meeting with a prospective client. A couple planning a party to celebrate their fiftieth anniversary," Bridgette elaborated. "Fiona likes to do one thing at a time whenever possible."

"Interesting." Moving the pad to one side, Hank flipped through his calendar. Since he'd joined the firm, three new accounts had come his way, with more in the offing. He wanted to give each his personal attention. That necessitated his going to each company and spending the better part of the day orienting himself about products, procedures and any little thing that might spark his imagination. "I'm kind of booked up for the next few weeks."

"Oh."

Disappointment dripped from the single word. It was a setup all right, he thought. But one he fully meant to take advantage of.

Hank turned the page and made a notation on the next day's page.

"Why don't I meet with you after-hours? Say tomorrow, about six-thirty?" He would have said today, except that he was driving up to Riverside to meet with the owner of Central Computers right after lunch. "There's a restaurant called McGonigle's on Newport Center Drive. Inside Fashion Island—"

"Don't bother with directions, I know where it is. We'll be there," Bridgette said with obvious delight.

Hank smiled to himself. He wondered what sort of story Bridgette was going to concoct to get Fiona to show up. "I'm looking forward to doing business with you, Ms. Reilly."

"It's Turner," Bridgette corrected. There was almost a wistful note as she confessed, "I'm married."

"The prettiest ladies usually are. Until tomorrow, then." Hank hung up.

"Until tomorrow." Bridgette sighed, her eyes fluttering shut as she let the receiver drop in the general vicinity of the telephone cradle. He could make her feel sexy just by saying goodbye. The man definitely had a gift. "Really, Fiona," she murmured, curling up on the sofa, "you've got to get this one before I decide to dump Brian and make a play for him my-self.''

''Are you talking to me?''

Startled, Bridgette looked up just as Fiona let her-self in the front door.

Muttering under her breath, Fiona wrestled the lock for possession of the key. Someday she was going to remember to oil that thing, she thought. It was one of the things on her endless list of things to do that she never got around to.

Bridgette was on her feet, trying hard to appear nonchalant. ''Um, no, I'm just talking out loud to myself.'' No time like the present to spring the trap, she decided. ''That was your gorgeous waiter on the phone. Hank,'' she added when Fiona said nothing.

Fiona stopped dead. ''He's not *my* waiter,'' she corrected. Her expression never changed, but her heart was doing handsprings. ''What did he want?'' She tried to sound disinterested, but she doubted she was fooling Bridgette. ''Did he forget something Sat-urday?''

''No, but apparently you did. He said he had men-tioned that advertising your business would get you the kind of customers you want.''

Fiona extracted a huge spiral notebook she kept on the bookshelf. Walking into the kitchen, she made herself comfortable at the counter. ''I changed my mind about advertising. I have the kind of customers I want. Paying ones.''

Bridgette sighed. ''All right, more of the same. *Lots* more of the same.'' She could see that Fiona was trying to ignore her. "Did you or did you not say you wanted to make a success of this business?"

To be a success at something had been Fiona's goal ever since she'd overheard her father declaring that she would never amount to anything or accomplish anything. She'd been determined to prove him wrong about *something* when it came to her.

"Yes, I said that, but—"

"Well, then, why are you dragging your feet about this?" Bridgette wanted to know. "Advertising can get you there."

They'd already danced around this pole. "Bridgette, advertising takes a lot of money. I do not have a lot of money. If you remember your basic geometry, if A equals B and B equals C, then A equals C. And thus I cannot advertise."

"I remember nothing about basic geometry other than the fact that Scott O'Hara had shoulders from here to Catalina and that he turned out to be a great kisser." Bridgette allowed herself to grin foolishly for a moment before getting back on the track. "And the only equation you should be interested in is that money makes money."

Pressing her lips together, Fiona prayed for strength. Bridgette certainly wasn't stupid, but there were times that she thought education had been a total waste in her sister's case. But then, she'd done very well for herself just by being Bridgette. Four beauty contest titles and a husband who was an independent producer of minor renown. Fiona knew Bridgette was only dabbling in her life because she was bored and felt she needed a hobby. Unfortunately for her, she was Bridgette's hobby.

"That's not an equation, that's a saying, and yes, I am familiar with it. I promise that as soon as I have some money to spare, I'll put it to work. Until then—" Calling an end to the conversation, Fiona opened the compilation of personal recipes she'd put together, looking for a specific one she'd mentioned to the Goldbergs.

Bridgette placed a hand over the open book, determined to get her attention. In her hand was a small rectangular piece of paper. She waved it in front of Fiona's face like a starting flag at a race. "You have the money."

Fiona stared at the moving piece of paper, but made no attempt to take it. "What's this?"

Exasperated, Bridgette took her sister's hand and thrust the paper at her.

"My God, Fiona, can't you recognize a blank check when you see one?" Bridgette blew out a breath.

"Yes, I recognize a blank check when I see one." Fiona looked up at her sister. "I want to know why I'm seeing one."

Though Fiona held it out to her, Bridgette refused to take the check back. "I want to help finance the business."

Bridgette had come to her two months ago, offering to pitch in after Fiona's assistant had gotten married and moved to San Francisco. Fiona had fully expected Bridgette to be tired of playing by now.

"Since when?"

"Since now. C'mon, Fiona," Bridgette pressed eagerly, as if she could see Fiona was weakening. "It's not like I had to mortgage my firstborn. We're more than comfortable. Brian keeps encouraging me to spend my money on anything I want to."

Fiona thought of one of her sister's typical shopping sprees. Bridgette shopped as if it were not only her calling in life, but her patriotic duty, as well. "You do. On clothes and jewels and—"

Bridgette cut her short, her voice serious. "I want to spend it on my sister. On a dream, all right? Brian has his world and he's always busy. For once, I want to be part of something that's exciting, that has a chance to grow."

Bridgette really meant that, Fiona thought. She saw the urgency, heard the unspoken plea. It was enough to shake the foundations of the world she lived in. Setting the book aside, she looked at Bridgette, compassion in her eyes. "I always thought you were in the center of everything that was exciting."

"What, you mean beauty contests?" Bridgette hooted. "After the thrill wore off, there was this gaping, hollow feeling that snapped me up. When we got married, I thought maybe that I could become part of what Brian was doing. Every time I ask, he just pats me on the head and gives me another charge card. It's not enough," she confided quietly. "I want to be part of something, Fiona, something that grows and needs to be nurtured. I can't really build this business," she said, gesturing around the kitchen.

"That takes your talent, your drive. But I can fund it." She looked at Fiona hopefully. "What do you say?"

It was the first time Bridgette had ever asked her for anything. There was no way she could turn her down. Especially when she was placing her pride on the line, as well.

"What can I say? All right."

Bridgette threw her arms around her. "Thanks. I'll be your silent partner."

Fiona laughed. Did Bridgette actually expect her to believe that? "That'll be the day."

But it was a warm feeling, knowing her sister was actually there for her.

This was a meeting, just a business meeting, Fiona told herself for the dozenth time as she looked around the inside of McGonigle's. The restaurant, decorated to resemble a turn-of-the-century English pub, was dimly lit. Finding her sister was out of the question, at least until after her eyes had acclimatized to the restricted light.

She hoped it wouldn't be impossible after that. Bridgette was always late. For once she hoped her sister wasn't running true to form. Fiona didn't relish the idea of having to face Hank alone.

There was no reason in the world to feel this agitated, as if every pore in her body was dilated and alert. So she would be seeing Hank again, so what? So he had kissed her and melted every bone in her body, putting them out of commission, so what?

She'd returned to normal again. Was functioning again. And there was absolutely no chance of history repeating itself. This meeting was taking place under the best of conditions. She'd be seeing Hank in a populated restaurant with her sister sitting by her side—if Bridgette would just turn up.

When she did, it would be the kind of situation Fiona knew she functioned best in. Shy by nature, she'd forced herself to develop people skills, to talk and be assertive and present herself well. When she met with a prospective client, she wasn't Fiona Reilly the loudly lamented runt of the litter; she was Fiona Reilly the sole owner of a growing catering firm.

She couldn't say that anymore, Fiona realized. There was a check in her purse that negated that claim. Bridgette was her partner now and would undoubtedly want a say in things, no matter what she'd insisted yesterday. Fiona knew Bridgette. It was going to be a daily struggle just to keep her sister from taking over. But it was a struggle Fiona knew she was up to. Bridgette had never intimidated her. She'd only been envious of Bridgette while they were growing up. But even that had fallen by the wayside after yesterday.

She supposed that in certain respects, she'd come a long way from that timid mouse her father always cowed. She could hold her own now in the world. As long as ''her own'' didn't involve the thought of a personal relationship with a man.

Little danger of that, Fiona mused, seeing a couple

in the corner booth, their heads together as if they were sharing some secret only they were privy to.

Damn, where *was* Bridgette?

She thought of yesterday again. Who would have ever thought that Bridgette had an insecure side to her? And that she actually envied her. Bridgette had gone on to confide that she's always envied her spirit, her tenacity. Up until now, Fiona had never considered that beauty might have its drawbacks, that it might make you lazy because everything came to you so effortlessly. Pampered, spoiled, Bridgette didn't know how to fight for things that mattered.

Live and learn, Fiona mused, still scanning the immediate area, hoping to find her sister.

The instant she made eye contact, her heart began to hammer wildly. Instead of Bridgette, she'd found Hank. And he was sitting alone.

Fiona had a bad feeling about this.

"May I help you?" The question came from behind her.

Turning, Fiona saw that a waitress was making the polite inquiry.

Yes, don't block the exit. Bracing, Fiona took a deep breath, then indicated Hank's table. "I'm meeting him," she murmured.

The waitress looked clearly impressed. "Lucky you. Right this way." Picking up a menu from the hostess table, she led the way to the rear of the restaurant.

Hank rose in his seat as Fiona approached. "I was beginning to think I was being stood up."

"That would be a first, I'm sure."

Fiona Reilly, businesswoman; Fiona Reilly, businesswoman. The mantra played itself over and over again in her brain to no avail. She felt her bones going even as she took her seat.

She'd been wrong about his looks; they were even better than she recalled. She spread the forest-green napkin on her skirt. *Bridgette, where the heck are you?*

She forced a smile to her lips. "I guess my sister hasn't arrived yet."

"Haven't seen her," Hank confirmed. And he had a sneaking suspicion that he wouldn't, but that was all right with him. Business or pleasure, it was Fiona he was interested in seeing.

The waitress returned to their table and paused for a moment, as if making up her mind. "Are you Fiona Reilly?" she finally asked.

Puzzled, Fiona nodded. "Yes, I am. Is anything wrong?"

The waitress smiled, pleased that she had guessed correctly. "Your sister said you'd be sitting with the best-looking man in the restaurant."

The sinking sensation in Fiona's stomach went down below sea level. "My sister?"

"Yes, she just called to say that you should go ahead without her. She's come down with the flu and won't be able to join you," the waitress recited, her eyes never leaving Hank, "but you shouldn't worry."

"We'll have two glasses of white wine, please,"

Hank ordered. "That'll give us time to look over the menu."

Fiona shut her eyes, mortified. *I'll get you for this, Bridgette. If it's the last thing I do, I'll get you.* When she opened them again, she found herself looking directly into Hank's.

"Is everything all right?" There was a very strange expression on her face, Hank thought, as if she'd been caught completely unaware, completely defenseless.

Annoyed with Bridgette, Fiona forgot to be nervous. "No, it's not. And it's going to get worse." She blew out a breath. How could Bridgette have done something so transparent? Had yesterday's brief moment of sharing been a ruse, too? A lie just to set her up for this? "No one in my family's ever gone to prison before."

"Prison?" He didn't follow her, but he was beginning to think that wasn't such an uncommon thing when it came to Fiona. Her mind seemed to hop from one thing to another. "Who's going to prison?"

"I am, after I kill Bridgette." She gathered her purse to her. Hank was probably dying to get out of this poorly set trap. "Look, I'm sorry, it's obvious that my sister set this whole thing up." She began to rise, only to have him place his hand on her arm, silently urging her to sit down again.

"As a matter of fact, she did. She said that you changed your mind about advertising your catering business."

Was he being kind, or did he really not see what

was going on? Hoping for the latter, Fiona clutched at the excuse he'd just offered. There was no way she could pull off a dignified exit otherwise.

"Well, yes, actually. I have been thinking about what you said." *Business, remember the business.* She leaned forward, fixing him with a serious look and trying very hard to appear the hardened, driven career woman. "Exactly what can you do for me?"

This was a switch, Hank thought. She'd been so dubious the other night. He smiled into her eyes. "More than you could possibly guess."

The next moment Hank was pushing his chair back in a vain attempt to escape the cascading water from the glass Fiona had accidentally knocked over.

Things were going from awkward to immensely humiliating. The expression on his face had unsettled Fiona. When she'd drawn back, she'd hit her elbow against the water glass. A flood aimed at his crotch was the result.

A bright shade of pink washed over her face. "I'm so sorry."

Without thinking, she hurriedly began wiping the damp area. When it dawned on her that she was being far more intimate than she'd ever intended, Fiona dropped the napkin. Pink turned to scarlet as she prayed for an earthquake. A small one just under her chair that would open up the earth and mercifully swallow her.

Hank bit his lip, but he wasn't quite successful in holding his laughter back. He picked up the napkin she'd dropped.

"That's okay, I can take it from here," he assured her. For a moment back there, he'd almost bought her serious act. But this, he knew, was the real Fiona. He found her far more preferable to the other. "Besides, it's only water. It'll dry and the pants'll be none the worse for it."

Which was more than she could say for herself. Whatever made her think that she could just talk to him as if he were like anyone else?

"Look, maybe we should hold off until Bridgette gets over her 'flu.'" And if she didn't have the flu, she was going to wish she had, Fiona promised her sister silently. She picked up her purse again, ready to flee. "I'm not any good at this."

"'This?'" he asked innocently.

Why was he torturing her like this? He knew what she meant. "Talking to men." *Talking to you when you look at me like that.*

Hank slipped his hand over hers. "Then don't think of me as one. And I'll try not to think of you as a beautiful woman. Deal?"

A half smile twisted her lips. She remained where she was despite her common sense, which told her to leave now, before she did something worse, like set him on fire. "You got the easy part."

She meant that, Hank thought. Just as she meant all the disparaging remarks she'd made about herself. He frowned. "Why do you do that?"

His frown had an odd, calming effect on Fiona's nerves, deadening them. She raised her chin in a gesture of defiance that was lost on her, but not on Hank.

"Do what?"

"Run yourself down like that?" Hank said. She didn't do it because she was fishing for compliments; that much he'd already figured out.

Fiona looked away. This was the last thing she wanted to discuss. With anyone, least of all with him. "I'm not running myself down. I'm just being realistic—and truthful."

The hell she was. Someone had clearly done a job on her. A lover? Hank wondered. She didn't strike him as the type to be in an abusive relationship, but he'd been wrong before. Morgan was the last person in the world he would have thought could fall victim to that trap, but she had. And remained in it for almost six months until she woke up one morning and realized how much better she could do for herself.

"Fiona, there's modesty and then there's myopia. Take it from me, you're a very attractive woman." In a certain light, she was even beautiful, he thought, but he knew she wasn't ready to believe that. "Especially where it counts."

And where had she heard that before? Fiona thought. Her mother had tried to comfort her with almost those exact words. Though well-meaning, her mother's weak assurances had never done any good.

"Right, spirit." Fiona said it bitterly, unable to cut the bad taste from her mouth. It dredged up too many bad memories for her. "Okay, let's you, my beautiful spirit and I get down to basics." All business now, she looked at him. "What kind of advertising did you have in mind for my company?"

Hank was tempted to comment on the trio she'd cited so sarcastically, but left it alone. He could appreciate her wanting to retreat to the topic that had originally been the excuse they had both used to be here.

"For starters," he told her, "TV."

"Starters?" she echoed. Advertising on television was the pinnacle, not the starting point. "My sister's last name is Turner, however, there is no relation to Ted. Translation—I haven't got the kind of money TV requires."

Hank knew there were ways of doing things. One of his old friends was down here, working at a station that broadcast out of Bedford. "I was thinking of local independent stations."

She shook her head. "Still too high."

"Very local," he emphasized.

"Think more in terms of a local puppet show, put on by first graders," she quipped, taking a sip of her wine. "Maybe kindergartners." Bad move, she realized. The wine went directly to her head. Very carefully, she set the glass down and waited for the room to refocus.

"If you flip around the local stations, you'll notice that a lot of people are doing their own advertising these days. It might look a little amateurish, but done right, it's not without its charm. After all, it doesn't have to be fancy to be good." She was looking at him doubtfully. Obviously she needed further persuasion, Hank thought. "The tastiest thing I ever had was my mother's rhubarb pie. Didn't look like much,

definitely had a bad name, but it tasted like heaven.
One taste and I was hooked. My dying request would
be to have a piece of that pie. Not fancy, just good.''
He looked at her significantly. ''Remember that.''

Fiona didn't know if she was reading too much
into what he was saying. Probably. The mind did
strange things when it was floating.

''All right.'' For the sake of argument, she went
along with it for the moment. ''Just how much 'not
fancy' can you get me for this amount?''

She took out the check Bridgette had given her
and very carefully wrote in an amount that she felt
she could live with. Bridgette would probably insist
that she take more, but she wasn't about to go deeply
into debt no matter who was lending her the money
or how desperately she wanted it.

Hank took the check from her and looked at it.
Though significant in her terms, in his it would mean
stretching things. A lot. But he did like a challenge.

''It's doable.'' For now, he handed her back the
check. ''Keep that handy,'' he advised. ''There's a
guy I'd like you to meet.'' He saw her expression.
''Why did you wince just now?''

''Sorry, conditioned response.'' Fiona tucked the
check away. ''My friends are always saying that to
me.'' She shrugged, not even knowing why she was
saying this to him. ''It seems that the world doesn't
like odd numbers. Like one.''

He appeared to study her for a moment. ''Do they
set you up on a lot of blind dates?''

She laughed to herself, toying with the stem of the

wineglass. She wasn't about to have any more until after she ate. "They try."

"But you don't go," he guessed.

She shook her head. "Too busy."

Hank had a hunch it wasn't that. "Lucky for me you weren't too busy tonight." He could see the waitress looking their way. He signaled for her to come over, then looked at Fiona. "Let's order, shall we?"

Every time he smiled at her like that, Fiona could feel a tidal wave washing over her, taking her breath away. She glanced at the menu, too flustered to focus on the actual words.

"What looks good to you?"

His smile widened. "I'd say you, but then you might run off again, so I won't." Humor played along his mouth as he lowered his eyes to the menu. "I like a good steak myself. Rare. Plain, but with flavor. Beats those fancy dishes every time."

Fiona had no idea what possessed her, but she took his declaration as a direct challenge.

6

"Oh, I don't know about that," Fiona countered.

The quizzical look on Hank's face had her continuing without drawing a breath. If there was anything she was confident about, it was her ability to make mouth-watering meals. Ever since she could see over the kitchen counter, she'd had a knack of taking mundane ingredients and creating culinary magic with them. It was a talent that she knew set her apart and one she took refuge in.

"I think I could whip up a dish or two that might just woo you away from your allegiance to meat and potatoes."

Hank steepled his fingers together as he studied her. The change amazed him. One moment, Fiona was in retreat; the next, she was serenely confident.

"Are you inviting me over for a home-cooked meal?"

That wasn't exactly what Fiona had meant. But then, how else could he have taken it? It did sound like an invitation.

"I—that is—" There was no graceful way to get out of this. Maybe she didn't altogether want to, she realized. Why else would she have set herself up like this?

"Because if you are," he continued, "I accept. I haven't had a decent home-cooked meal since I left home."

"You can't cook?" She had no idea why that surprised her. Maybe it was because he seemed so completely self-sufficient to her. She pictured him being capable in any given situation.

One side of his mouth rose in a half smile as Hank thought of one particular messy fiasco he'd engaged in. He'd tried to make stew the way his mother did and wound up with burnt chips permanently soldered onto the bottom of his only pot.

"Only to survive. It's not one of my major talents. Besides, there's never enough time for it." He worked late at the office and availed himself of take-out or thirty-minute deliveries to avoid puttering in the kitchen. During rare, creative moments, he bought cold cuts and made sandwiches.

Since a great deal of her time was spent in the kitchen, coaxing along new creations or working with old, familiar recipes, Fiona couldn't imagine not having the time to cook.

"For me, there's always enough time to cook. Cooking relaxes me."

It had the opposite effect on him. Especially when pots boiled over. He would have thought that since Fiona's line of work required a great deal of cooking, the last thing she'd want to do when she was off was prepare a meal. "Even under pressure?"

"Especially under pressure." That was when she was at her best, exhilarated by the challenge. "I'm not very good at other things, but in the kitchen— well, in the kitchen it doesn't matter how tall I am, or if I'm wearing any makeup. Seasonings don't care what you look like, only how creative you are."

His expression was bemused. "I wasn't aware that seasonings had opinions at all."

She'd talked too much, Fiona thought ruefully. "You're laughing at me again."

He reached for her hand.

"No, I'm not. I'm not laughing, I'm smiling." His eyes touched hers warmly. "With you."

"But I'm not smiling." Even as she said it, she struggled to keep her mouth from curving in response to his expression. Just being around him made her want to smile.

"Then you should be." His hand closed over hers. "It makes your face glow."

It took effort not to shift beneath his gaze. His compliments made her feel awkward, even as she welcomed them. She'd never really had to deal with compliments before.

"That's probably sweat. I've been on the go all day," she told him, "and I haven't had a chance to cool down yet."

She had hurried here directly from a meeting with another prospective client, unable to stop at home to change the way she had planned. Best-laid plans died when meetings ran over. She'd instinctively learned never to hurry a would-be client along. Usually, the affair they wanted catered was of utmost importance to them. That necessitated kid-glove treatment. Rushing was not part of the deal.

Very slowly, his eyes still on hers, Hank rubbed his thumb along her palm. The tiny action immediately awakened every nerve ending in her body.

"Then don't cool down. I like you this way."

"Sweaty?"

"Glowing," he corrected.

Was it her, or was the room suddenly growing even darker than it had been when she'd first entered? Darker and hotter.

"Are you ready to order?" the waitress asked.

The soft, cocooning darkness ebbed away a little as she looked up at the waitress.

"Absolutely." Picking up her menu, Fiona quickly scanned the two long pages and made an arbitrary choice. It didn't really matter what she ordered; she doubted that she would actually taste the food anyway. Nerves had disintegrated her taste buds.

He definitely made her nervous, Hank thought. He smiled to himself as he waited for Fiona to finish ordering. She both aroused and stimulated him without, he had a strong suspicion, meaning to do either. She was too busy trying to retreat.

Whether it was a horse he wasn't supposed to ride or an account that appeared to be out of reach, he'd always been a sucker for a challenge and Fiona Reilly had all the makings of a very stimulating, very intriguing challenge. It might be interesting to be instrumental in releasing the woman he sensed was trapped within that proper, delicate exterior she turned to the world.

He knew what they said about still waters.

Fiona sighed, too full to move.

It was rare that she actually sat down for a meal and rarer still that it wasn't at her own table. It was nice to have someone else do the work for a change, even though the sauce was a little too tangy for her taste. Tangy or not, she could still appreciate all the work that had gone into the preparation.

Finishing the meal was one thing. It would have been rude to leave it half eaten. But ordering the chocolate mud-pie had been nothing short of sheer indulgence on her part.

She slid the last crumb into her mouth, savoring it. It had been delicious.

Still, like a sinner after the fact, she murmured guiltily, "I shouldn't have had that dessert."

Hank had watched her eat with pleasure. Unlike some women he knew who picked at their food, Fiona ate as if she were enjoying every bite. "Why, afraid you'll actually tip the hundred-pound mark on the bathroom scale?"

He made her sound like some fragile little doll. "I weigh more than a hundred pounds."

Hank shook his head. He knew better. "Didn't feel that way to me when I caught you in my arms the other night."

The mere mention of the incident had long fingers

of warmth moving all through her, prodding Fiona in places that had no business being prodded. Especially when there was nothing she could do about it.

Fiona shrugged carelessly, as if to dismiss the subject. "Maybe you've been working out too much and your muscles got in the way."

"Maybe," he agreed playfully. He signed his name on the credit card slip, then laid down the pen. "Ready to go?"

She began to move back her chair. "You might have to carry me."

Hank rather liked the thought. His eyes teased her. "Oh, I think I can bear up to it if necessary." Rising, he pulled back her chair for her and helped her to her feet. The nervous look was back in her eyes, he noticed. A definite challenge. "By the way, when should I come over?"

She'd almost stopped midstep, but managed to keep walking. "Come over?" she echoed. When had she invited him to her house?

Taking her arm, he guided her to the door. The fact that every female head in the establishment watched his progress was not lost on her.

"For that home-cooked meal," he was saying. "Don't tell me you're backing out. My taste buds couldn't stand the disappointment."

Fiona had hoped that he had forgotten about that.

It had been a definite slip on her part. She might have known better. Murphy's law. Now that he actually was calling her on it, Fiona felt herself fumbling inwardly. It wasn't that she minded cooking for someone, she didn't. Doing so gave her a great deal of pleasure. But on a personal basis, she had only cooked for friends, or for Bridgette and her family.

Just the thought of cooking for Hank tied her up in a multitude of unmanageable tiny, tight knots. Though she still didn't believe that this was anything more than an amusing way to kill time for him, that didn't stop her from wanting to impress him.

Mentally, Fiona quickly reviewed her schedule for the next few days. She was going to be busy, but Friday night was free.

As usual, she thought sarcastically.

"Friday night's probably inconvenient for you," she guessed out loud. She was prepared to be told that he couldn't make it.

He surprised her. "No, it's wide open." He held the door for her, waiting until she passed through first.

Fiona felt an icy chill zip over her, followed by enough heat to melt a mountain of ice. He was actually going to come over.

"You don't have a date?" She found that almost impossible to believe.

She was trying her damnedest to wheedle out of this, he thought. Hank looked into her eyes. The light in them made his pulse quicken just a little. This was something he intended to explore further.

"I do now."

"A date?" No, no, that wasn't what she'd meant at all. This wasn't going to be a date, it was going to be a lesson, a business meeting with food. Panic hit her with the force of an anvil dropping on her foot "You mean, you're actually coming over to my house for dinner?"

"That's exactly what I mean. You can't renege now, Fiona," he warned playfully. "Your reputation's at stake." He outlined the evening for her. "You make the food, I bring the wine. We eat, talk…whatever—"

Fiona swallowed, calling herself an idiot for being such a mouse. "'Whatever'?"

They were standing at the foot of the steps that led to the sidewalk. The early evening breeze was playfully tugging at the ends of her hair, making them swirl around her face. Hank combed them away from her face with his fingers.

"Whatever," he repeated with a soft smile. "It means that the evening's wide open. We can do whatever we want. You're not afraid, are you?"

"No." The denial popped out before she could stop it. Before she allowed herself to be truthful with him.

Hank pretended to take her at her word, though he could see she was lying. "Good."

But Fiona was afraid, afraid of making even more of a fool of herself than she had before. Afraid of not being able to retreat when she wanted to. Invention, born in the wake of necessity, had her reconnoitering. "Um, why don't I bring the meal to your place instead?"

It made no difference to Hank where they got together so long as they did, but he didn't see why she why was pressing for the change in venue. "Why?"

She thought fast. "Because then it would seem more like catering that way. If I serve you in your dining room, maybe it might help you come up with something to help with the advertising."

She'd inadvertently hit upon the way he operated, he thought. All right, he saw no reason to try to dissuade her. Her place, his place, it was all one and the same to him. Whatever was meant to happen between them would happen no matter where she was serving.

"Good idea," he agreed.

Fiona sighed, savoring her minor victory for a few moments before wondering if he had some ulterior motive for agreeing. He'd been awfully quick to agree.

Yes, Fiona thought the following Friday as she packed the last of the dinner she'd prepared into the van, it was a very good idea to do it this way. Coming to him, she could leave anytime she thought she should. If he came over to her place, she couldn't just pack up and leave when she felt it was time. She'd be stuck. And then who knew what might happen?

This was a much smarter move for her.

Hank startled her by opening the door before she had a chance to ring.

"I saw you pull up," he explained, answering the unspoken question in her eyes. "Here, let me help you with that.'' He took an unusually large, covered rectangular pan from her. ''What is this? Feels heavy.''

Fiona reached into the rear of the van and took out another pan, a smaller one than the one he was holding. ''A little of this, a little of that.''

Her smile, Hank thought, was positively mysterious.

He led the way into his kitchen. Out of the corner of his eye, he saw her looking around as she followed. ''This would have been easier for you at your house.''

He was right, but she stuck by her guns, unwilling to tell him the real reason she was doing it this way. ''Yes, but then you couldn't get the feel of having something catered.'' She set the pan down on the first flat surface she came to in the kitchen.

It was a country-style kitchen, wide and airy. Perfect for working in. It seemed wasted on him, she thought.

Fiona went back to the van for the next round of pans. He was right beside her.

''You said you wanted to get to know as much about my business as possible,'' she reminded him. ''This will give you the customer perspective.''

''I already have the server perspective,'' he teased, taking a large pot this time.

She avoided his eyes. ''Yes, thanks to my mistake,'' she agreed.

''It turned out for the best. I wouldn't be anticipating a great deal of 'this and that,''' he added, deliberately using her vague terminology, "if you hadn't pounced on me."

Turning the first pan sideways, she set down the second one and then moved aside so that he could do the same. "I didn't pounce—exactly. Besides, it was your own fault for being as tall as Alex."

"Which reminds me, what are you doing these days for a replacement?" Though she'd originally asked if he'd be interested in helping her again, she'd never taken him up on it. He'd just assumed that Alex's injury hadn't been as bad as first thought.

"I contacted the agency. I really do act rationally, given the right amount of time."

Amusement curved his mouth. "Never crossed my mind to think you didn't."

She loved his smile, Fiona thought. It seemed to curl right into the very heart of her, spreading tongues of fire in all directions. It made her tingle if she looked at him long enough.

Which was why it was important not to. She couldn't just stand here in the middle of his kitchen, tingling. She was supposed to be behaving like a professional, not like an auburn vibrator.

It looked as if she was moving in, Hank thought, glancing around. There were enough covered pots, pans and containers littering every available space in his kitchen to hold a garage sale on kitchenware.

"All this for one meal?" he marveled. He should have insisted she do this at her place. She was going to far too much trouble.

"It's a potpourri. Besides…" she sniffed, adjusting the oven temperature. "Don't question an artist."

He laughed, holding up his hands. "I wouldn't dream of it."

Hank watched her move around, poetry in a pair of jeans. He was tempted to lace his hands around her small waist and bring her to him, saying the hell with the meal. All the sustenance he needed was located just above her chin.

But he had a feeling she wouldn't be pleased to hear that right now. Not after all this preparation.

He hovered, not knowing what to do with himself as she worked. "Can I do anything to help?"

She raised an incredulous eyebrow. "I thought you couldn't really cook."

"I can't." He saw no point in lying. "But I'm dynamite when it comes to handing things like spoons or saltshakers." Hank winked at her conspiratorially. "Try me."

There was nowhere to duck to get out of range. The wink went straight into her system. "All you have to do is sit back and enjoy it."

His smile was lazy, sexy, as his eyes drifted over her. "I'm doing that already."

No, this wasn't going to work at all. She needed him in another room, somewhere where she wasn't so acutely aware of his every glance, his every breath. "I move pretty fast—maybe you'd better stay out of my way." She gestured toward the next room, hoping he'd take the hint.

It fell on deaf ears. "Uh-uh, the deal is that I watch

you, remember? Get the feel of all the effort you put into something.'' He was throwing her own words back at her. "It'll give the ad more of an honest feel.''

She'd never thought of ads as being particularly honest. The good ones were catchy, but that was all. "Why can't you just make something up?''

Why was she so anxious to get rid of him? Hank wondered. Was she afraid that he might see something he shouldn't? Some secret recipe that had been handed down through generations? Suddenly it was important to him that she trust him.

"It's better if I believe it.''

She sighed. "All right, but it'll take longer this way.''

He shrugged, making himself comfortable at the kitchen table. "I'm not going anywhere.''

A little more than an hour later, Hank leaned back on the dining room chair. If it wasn't so damn impolite, he would have been tempted to unbutton the top button of his jeans. They'd gone from comfortable to tight in less than sixty minutes. He'd done his best not to overindulge, but Fiona had made everything look so good—and taste so good—that he couldn't help himself.

Fiona eyed him, waiting for a response. Though he had eaten and they'd talked on a variety of subjects, he hadn't really said anything about the food. It seemed ridiculous to her that his approval should matter so much to her, but it did. She wanted it. Deserved it, she amended.

"Well?"

Hank inclined his head, a contender taking his defeat with grace. "I stand corrected. Everything I had tonight was beyond description."

That didn't sound encouraging as far as the future of their business association went. "I thought you were so good with words."

"I am, but it's going to take time to find the ones that will do your culinary skills justice. Where did you learn to cook like that?"

"Watching our housekeeper, Mavis. She was a whiz in the kitchen and she let me experiment when no one was around. I told you, cooking relaxes me. I like doing it."

He nodded. "It certainly shows." Ideas began materializing in his brain. "Fiona, with the right management, you could be in such demand, you wouldn't have a moment to call your own."

She grinned. That would certainly prove her father's prophecy wrong. "I could live with that."

He looked at the dish she picked up. "That sauce, you didn't just make that, you created it, right?"

It pleased her that he had guessed right. She nodded as she stacked the dishes. "Right. My own recipe."

He was on his feet, helping her, making plans. He'd already come up with a logo for her. That small stick figure balancing the wedding cake had taken on a life of its own. Charmed by it, Fiona had taken it to a printer to have it embossed on her business card.

"We could bottle that. Sell it to stores or restaurants. Better yet—" Excitement began to pulse through him. Moving around so that he was in front of her, Hank took hold of her shoulders, trying to make Fiona see that she was standing on the brink of something very big. "I'm thinking expansion, I'm thinking a chain. Maybe even a franchise."

He was getting swept up in his enthusiasm. She hadn't thought he could be so animated. Fiona placed a hand on his shoulder before he got completely carried away.

"Just think advertising. *Local* advertising," she emphasized. "We'll take quantum leaps later." It was nice that he had such faith in her, but she had always been a realist at bottom and she wanted to make perfectly sure that each step she took was reinforced and secure.

Hank placed his hand over hers, forgetting the bonanza he was envisioning for a moment and concentrating instead on the woman behind it.

"Let yourself go a little, Fiona," he urged. "Dream."

Self-conscious again, Fiona pulled away. "I'd better get these dishes washed before I put them in the van." She stared down at the plate. "This sauce is almost impossible to work with once it dries."

She wasn't worried about the sauce, she was backing away. It was like a dance, Hank thought. They moved forward, they moved back, always in circles.

He was beginning to think that he might like to try moving in a straight line for a change.

Following her into the kitchen, Hank brought the rest of the dishes with him. Though very organized in appearance, the kitchen was besieged by a battalion of pots and pans.

Fiona took the plates he was holding. She nodded toward the dining room. She needed to be alone for a few minutes, to get her bearings back. To remember that she was his client and that their relationship had to remain strictly professional. To want something otherwise was just stupid. At the very least, it was asking for trouble.

"If you were the client, you wouldn't be doing that. Why don't you—"

He wasn't about to leave. She was going to have to get over whatever it was that seemed to spook her around him.

"Maybe it's not my place to ask this, but just why are you so skittish? Most women don't mind being around me. They certainly don't act as if I were a time bomb, about to explode in their faces at any second."

She didn't owe him an explanation, but the part of her that had been teased mercilessly, that had been ridiculed and belittled until there had been nothing left of her self-esteem except tatters, didn't want him to believe that he was responsible for her reaction.

"It's not you, it's me."

That was the most banal of cop-outs. He leaned

his hip against the sink and waited. "That's not enough of an explanation."

Someone else might have shrugged and said, "Take it or leave it," but Fiona wasn't someone else. She was far too sensitive to be insensitive to someone else.

She started to wash the dishes. Her voice was only a little louder than the rushing stream of water when she began to talk. Hank had to listen close to hear her.

"When I was fifteen years old, I had a crush on Jason Greeley. At the time I thought he was the most gorgeous thing on two feet. I was sure I would die from loving him. He was in a couple of my classes and all I could do was just stare at him like some lovesick puppy. One day, out of the blue, he walked up to my locker, took me in his arms and kissed me." She took a deep breath, as if to shield herself from what she was about to say next. "My head spun and I swore I heard music.

"It was a short song. After he kissed me, he walked away and I saw him put his hand out to my cousin, Jimmy. Jimmy gave him a five-dollar bill and Jason smirked and said, 'See, I told you I could kiss anyone on a dare, even her.'"

Fiona blinked. It was stupid to still feel the pain after all this time. But she did. "I could have died." She looked up at Hank. "The worst part of it was that I was stupid enough to think that someone who looked like Jason would have actually been attracted to me."

"There's nothing wrong with you," he insisted.

"No, there isn't," she agreed. "But I'm not the kind of woman who attracts men like Jason." She knew her pluses and she knew her limitations. "Or men like you. I'm solid, dependable and great in an emergency, but I'm meat and potatoes, not caviar. The Jasons of the world want caviar." And she was never going to let anyone hurt her like that again.

Hank began to understand. "I already told you, I have a weakness for meat and potatoes. Just because I discovered that I like fancy cream sauce doesn't change that. Meat and potatoes are always satisfying, always good." His eyes skimmed along her face. He wanted to get her to see what he saw. "Can I stop playing client now?"

Fiona could feel herself begin to feel uneasy again. "Why?"

His smile was slow, mellow, comforting. It amazed her that the same expression could be so many different things, evoke so many different emotions from her. "Because I want to help you with the dishes."

She laughed, relieved. "I won't argue."

"Good." He picked up a towel and began to dry the dishes she had done. "And while we're doing them, let me tell you what else I have in mind for your company." For now, Hank thought, he was going to concentrate on the business end. The other part would come along naturally enough if he was just patient. "You're going to bless the day you met me," he promised.

One thing was for sure, Fiona thought. She certainly wasn't going to forget it.

7

The sound of a doorbell wedged its way between the seams of the perfectly lovely dream she was having. With each peal the sound became stronger and the dream dissolved a little more, becoming misty until the very shape of it eluded her.

Against her will, Fiona woke up. As her brain cleared, she vainly tried to hang on to unrecognizable, elusive fragments. All she could remember, even now, was that the dream had left her with a feeling of euphoria that all but vibrated through her body.

With a surrendering sigh, she sat up. She needed to pull herself together. Fiona glanced toward the clock out of habit, not bothering to focus on it. Whatever time it said, it was too early. The Goldbergs had given her carte blanche yesterday, saying they wanted to spare no expense, asking only that the affair be memorable. They were an adorable couple, still affectionate after all these years, but they had laid a heavy burden on her shoulders with their trust. She'd been up until the wee hours of the morning, putting together what eventually amounted to a killer menu. That had required a great deal of cooking and sampling. And a great deal of discarding.

She'd collapsed into bed sometime around two, expecting to sleep like a dead person. But the dream she'd had had been far from restful.

Hank.

It had been about Hank, she realized suddenly. And it had been erotic. That was all she could remember. It was more than she needed right now.

The ringing wouldn't go away.

Fiona tried to think. This was the first Saturday in a month that she didn't have a wedding to cater, so the person ringing her doorbell couldn't be Bridgette. Besides, she usually had to call to get Bridgette to show up. No one liked to sleep in the way Bridgette did.

It was probably some neighborhood child, collecting for his school or club or, worse yet, someone from a religious sect, determined to convert her. Fiona decided to ignore whoever it was; she lay down again and pulled the comforter over her head.

The telephone rang.

Technology was ganging up on her. Throwing off the comforter, she reached for the telephone and pulled it closer to her. She propped herself up on her elbow and mumbled a drowsy, "Hello?"

"Answer your doorbell, Fiona."

She sat up, instantly awake and combing her fingers through her hair in an attempt to look presentable. As if he could see her through the wires.

"Hank?" How did he know someone was ringing her doorbell? she wondered. "Where are you?"

"On your doorstep." He'd been all but leaning on her doorbell. After five minutes, he'd become concerned that something was wrong. Her car was still in the driveway, so he knew she hadn't left for a job. "I'm calling from my cell phone. If you look out your window, you can see me."

Receiver in hand, Fiona scrambled off the bed and looked out the window. Hank had backed away from the door and was standing in her driveway. He waved when he saw her. Suddenly feeling as if she were back in her dream, Fiona waved back.

"Open the front door," he said into his phone. "I have something to show you."

With the phone cradled against her shoulder and neck, Fiona was already shoving her arms into the robe she kept flung across the foot of her bed.

She caught a glimpse of herself in the mirror. The robe had seen better days. As had she, she thought ruefully. There was no way she could let him see her looking like this. Right now, she was two steps removed from a bag woman.

Leaping over a cookbook she'd dropped on the floor, she made it to her closet in three steps. "Just give me a minute to put something on, all right?"

"Don't tell me you sleep in the nude, Fiona. My heart couldn't take it."

Fiona almost dropped the receiver. Flustered, but with a smile growing in the wake of his words, she tossed it onto her bed.

"Wait," she ordered, raising her voice so he could hear her. She grabbed the first pair of shorts that looked presentable. Someday, she was going to get around to doing a proper load of laundry, she thought. But someday obviously wasn't going to be today.

She heard a faint, "Yes, ma'am," coming from the receiver.

Fiona could have sworn the words were followed by a chuckle. Why that should bring a warm flush racing through her body didn't make sense but she didn't have time to analyze it.

Barefoot, Fiona tied the ends of a worn T-shirt around her middle and hurried down the stairs. Velcro materialized, insisting on playing tag with her. The cat bounded down the stairs just ahead of her. Fiona held onto the banister, afraid that she'd go rolling down the stairs as she tried to avoid squashing the cat.

"S-scat," she hissed.

True to form, Velcro ignored her.

"You can be replaced with a stuffed animal, you know," Fiona warned, striding toward the door.

The animal merely meowed her contempt, taking her post by the door as if she wanted to know firsthand who was invading her domain this early in the morning.

"Hi," she murmured.

"Hi," Hank echoed, walking in. She looked tousled and absolutely delectable, he thought, turning to look at her. Her eyes were still swollen from the last remnants of sleep. He couldn't help wondering what it would be like, waking up to find her beside him, looking like that in the morning. "Sorry if I got you out of bed."

"Oh, you didn't—" she began, then thought better of the protest. She probably looked as if Velcro had dragged her around by all the back fences in town. "Yes, you did, but it's okay. I should have been up hours ago." Velcro was wrapping herself around his leg and digging in, just as she had done the first time he'd come over. This time, though, Hank didn't even seem to notice. He was probably used to that kind of ardent female attention, she thought, gingerly removing the cat and picking her up. "I don't usually sleep in this late, but it was a long night."

"Working?" Hank scratched Velcro's head. The cat purred as if she had died and gone to heaven.

Amazed by Velcro's reaction, Fiona nodded. "Trying to find just the right menu for this couple's golden wedding anniversary."

A low whistle of admiration left his lips. "Fifty years with the same person. Now that's what I call commitment."

She had a hunch that the only commitment he made was to his work. And who could blame him? He could have a different woman every night without any effort if he wanted to.

"Yes, it is. I guess that sort of thing is kind of rare these days," Fiona agreed.

"Oh, I don't know. My parents have been married thirty-five years. I guess it kind of helps to live on a ranch. Whenever they had an argument, there was a lot of space for them to retreat to until they got over whatever it was that had set them off in the first place.''

He'd had good, kind parents who loved each other, she thought enviously. ''Sounds a bit simpler than psychiatrists and marriage counselors.''

''Cheaper, too.'' He winced as Velcro's paw brushed against his knuckles. ''You might think about trimming her nails.''

''Sorry.'' She moved the cat out of range. ''I can lock her up in another room if you'd like.''

''No, that's okay. Maybe she'll get used to me.'' Hank turned to look at Fiona, feeling guilty now for having come over so early. But he knew that she'd want to see what he'd brought over. He cupped her chin in his hand, studying her face. ''Did you get any sleep at all?''

''Not much,'' she confessed. ''It felt like I was dreaming the minute I closed my eyes. I feel more exhausted now than when I went to bed.''

''Nightmare?'' he guessed.

''No,'' she said emphatically. Curiosity entered his eyes. ''Actually, it was about you.'' Fiona bit her lip. ''I probably shouldn't have said that.''

The lady, he thought, was refreshingly honest.

The smile on his lips curled all through her, nudging its way into every open space. ''Oh, I don't know,'' he said.

He toyed with the ends of her hair, standing much

too close. She should have held on to Velcro in self-defense, she thought.

"Was it a good dream?" he asked after a beat.

She lowered her eyes, suddenly embarrassed. When was she going to learn to think before she spoke? "I don't know. I can't remember."

She remembered, all right. If she didn't, she wouldn't be blushing. He was tempted to coax the details out of her. Hank raised her chin until their eyes met.

"Maybe we can do something to refresh your memory after you take a look at page two in the entertainment section." He held up the newspaper he'd brought for her perusal.

"Why, what's in it?" She had absolutely no clue what there might be in the newspaper that Hank would think she'd be interested enough in seeing to drive all the way over here.

Taking the newspaper from him, she turned to the page he'd specified. She honed in on the article quickly enough and scanned it. Her mouth dropping open in surprise when she saw her name, Fiona went back to the beginning of the piece and read the short article carefully this time. It was written by a food critic. And it was all about the party Fiona had catered the weekend before. When she finished reading, she had more questions than she'd had to begin with.

Hank watched in silent fascination as disbelief, joy and a host of other emotions moved over her face. Unable to contain himself, he took the paper from her.

"Here, let me read it to you," he volunteered. Her fingers, he noticed, were lax as she surrendered the paper. "'I never thought I'd be taking a busman's holiday,'" he began, reading out loud, "'but there's something I feel I have to share with you. If you ever find yourself entertaining more than two for dinner, it might behoove you to look up a Ms. Fiona Reilly.'" He stole a look at her. "'The lady is the owner of a quaint little catering company called Painless Parties. Believe me, there is nothing quaint about the food she will bring to your table…'"

Fiona placed her hand on his arm. Hank stopped reading and looked at her. "Did you do this?"

He held up the paper for her verification. "It says right here it was written by Terrance Gilbert." He pointed to the byline.

"I didn't ask if you wrote this, I asked if you *did* this." Fiona knew by the look on his face that she was right. Somehow, Hank had had a hand in this article. "Did you bribe this Terrance Gilbert to write the article?"

Hank laughed at the mere thought of anyone telling Terrance what to write. Terrance Gilbert was the most opinionated person he knew, barring maybe his sister.

"If you knew Terry, you wouldn't ask that question. He considers himself above things like bribery. And he's pretty much of a food snob. But yes, I do know him and it so happens that he's friends with one of Mrs. Harrison's sons-in-law," he explained, mentioning the name of the woman who'd had the party catered. "We had lunch the other day. We were talking and your name came up. He mentioned the dinner he'd attended and I mentioned that you could use the publicity. In the trade, this is called serendipity." He handed the paper back to her. "I thought you might want to save this. It's a damn nice write-up."

"Yes." Fiona looked at the page. "It is."

"My guess is that it should go a long way in bringing you some more business. People actually take Terry to heart. But then, they don't know him the way I do."

Fiona raised a brow in silent query.

"We went to school together. I saved his butt once."

And now Gilbert was returning the favor, she thought. For reasons she couldn't quite pin down yet, it made her feel closer to Hank. No matter what he said to the contrary, he'd called in a personal favor to help her. Didn't that put them half a step beyond just working professionals?

As did his showing up on her doorstep, she realized a moment later.

The telephone rang just then. "I'd say that might be someone who just read his morning paper." Pleased with himself, he nodded toward the telephone. "Why don't you go and answer it?"

Torn between wanting to bask in the glow generated by knowing he'd done her a personal favor and wanting to take advantage of the result of that favor, she finally held up her hand.

"Wait right here." Fiona bent over the sofa to get to the telephone.

Her shorts rode up high on her leg, giving Hank an unobstructed view of perfectly sculpted, firm thighs. He continued looking, unabashed. "I'm in no hurry to go anywhere."

Three phone calls, all coming on the heels of one another, went by before Fiona finally had a chance to talk to him again.

Turning to address Hank, she found him sitting on the floor, scratching the cat behind the ears. Velcro was utterly submissive.

"I've never seen her behave like that with a stranger before."

"All she wants is a little attention, don't you, girl?" The cat was on her back, her feet straight up in the air as she absorbed the magic coming from his fingertips. Fiona had a bizarre urge to purr and emulate her pet.

"Don't we all," Fiona murmured. When he looked at her, a bemused expression on his face, she knew she'd misspoken again. "About the article," she added quickly, sliding her hands over the creased page. "I have no idea what to say. Thank you doesn't begin to cover it."

"No, it doesn't," he agreed. Patting the cat, he set her upright and turned his attention to Fiona.

She wasn't sure just what to make of the intense look in his eyes. All she knew was that it was undoing her. "Right, the check." She went to get it.

It surprised her that Hank still hadn't taken it from her, even though they had met in his office several times already. Each meeting was conducted after-hours because of his heavy schedule. She didn't mind adjusting her time around him, but she didn't like feeling as if she were in debt to him.

But he stopped her before she could find her purse. "For the time being, I have a different form of payment in mind."

Though she still couldn't remember the details, her dream had left her feeling tingly and vulnerable. The effect intensified as he looked at her with what her grandmother's generation had referred to as "bedroom eyes."

"Such as?" she heard herself whisper.

His answer wasn't what she expected. "Collins Walker is having their annual party in a couple of weeks. Since I'm the new guy, it's my job to find a suitable caterer to handle the details." He tugged on the knot in her T-shirt. "Know anyone I can use?"

"Very funny." She was grateful that the conversation had turned to business. "How many people are going to be there and what would you like?"

He was quiet for a second, seeming to do a mental tally. "Roughly three hundred and what I personally would like is if you told me your dream."

So much for taking refuge in business. He was making those strange things happen inside her again. "I already told you that I couldn't remember." Although now there were snippets whizzing through her brain, teasing her like a memory that had faded but wasn't quite gone yet.

"And I volunteered to help you try." He took her into his arms. "Does this help?"

Settling against him felt like heaven. A very particularly accelerated heaven, where pulses raced alongside hearts. "My circulation, yes. My memory, no."

"How about this, does this help?"

Even as he spoke, Hank lowered his mouth to hers, skimming his lips along hers. Her sharp intake of breath excited him. No more skimming, no more teasing. He slanted his mouth against hers, drawing in her sweetness, exchanging it for passion.

The battle was lost before a single weapon was discharged. Before a single weapon was even drawn. Defenseless, she twined her arms around his neck, her body allowing itself to be molded to his.

Fiona couldn't fathom why he would want to kiss her.

Maybe the thought that she was resisting prompted him, she didn't know. And right now, she didn't care. All she cared about was that he *was* kissing her. She had never felt like this about anyone before. And in all likelihood, never would again.

She took his breath away, Hank realized. There was no other way to describe it. This deceptive-looking little slip of a thing, with her eagerness, her verve, stole the very air from his lungs. Pulling his head back, he was silent for a moment, trying to get his bearings as he looked at her. Very slowly, he ran his hands along her back, the very feel of her comforting him.

And then he smiled at her. "Wow, I don't know about you, but that's certainly going to set me off dreaming for quite some time to come." Very gently, he brushed back a lock of her hair. "You're not at all what you seem, Fiona Reilly."

She blinked, not knowing what he meant by that. "I'm not?"

"No, you're not. You're not nearly as reserved, as straitlaced as you try to pretend."

She tried to withdraw, but it was too late for that. She was his for the taking and she knew that he knew. But what he didn't know, she thought, was what was inside her.

"I don't want people to think I'm standoffish. I'm not," she insisted. "I'm...afraid." The admission wasn't an easy one to make.

Hank tried to understand. As far as he remembered, he'd never been afraid of anything. Except maybe thunder, but he'd been five at the time.

"Of what, Fiona?" Holding her to him, he searched her eyes, looking for his answer there. "Of me?"

She nodded; it was simpler that way. Fiona was unable to put into words that it wasn't him she was afraid of, but what she felt for him. Wondrous though it was, this feeling would get out of hand and take over her life. And then, when he'd satisfied his curiosity—or whatever it was that had him dallying with her like this—and left her, she wouldn't be able to bear it.

"Don't be afraid," he coaxed softly. He framed her face with his hands. How could she think herself plain? The light in her eyes made her beautiful. "Don't ever be afraid of me."

But she was, he thought, and he didn't know what to do about it.

"Do you believe in chemistry, Fiona?"

Her eyes narrowed. "Chemistry?"

"You know, that funny thing that draws two people together while repelling two others. I believe in chemistry," he told her seriously. "More important than that, I believe that when there's chemistry between two people, they owe it to themselves to explore it."

For the first time humor played along her lips. "In the name of science?"

His gut tightened as desire flooded through him. "In the name of any damn thing you want."

And then, because she tempted him in a way he'd never been tempted before, he forgot that he wanted to take her to meet someone. He forgot everything, except that he wanted her, wanted this woman who was a combination of innocence and sex, of laughter and seriousness. He wanted her in the worst way.

In the best way that a man could want a woman.

He kissed her again. And again, slanting his mouth over hers first gently, then with a growing urgency, and finally with passion. Holding her to him, feeling her hands as they first timidly, then with growing confidence and hunger, swept along his back. He savored the way her body trembled against his.

Savored, too, that his own body was trembling in awed anticipation. He wanted to make love with her. He wanted to show her that she *was* beautiful. Beautiful to him.

And then the phone rang, shattering its way into their private world of two.

Fiona wanted to ignore it, to shut it out and focus instead on the heat that was traveling through her body at the speed of a racing train. His lips were doing such wonderful things to the pulse in her throat. Fiona gripped his shoulders as her head fell back, her skin eager for the feel of his mouth.

"Don't you think you should answer that?" he asked.

It took her a moment to understand the words. Another to focus.

"Right. Sure."

And a third moment to feel the bitter sting of disappointment as his words, as their meaning, penetrated. Didn't he want to make love with her? She'd all but waved the white flag in his face, all but laid herself out on a serving tray for his pleasure.

For *her* pleasure.

She flushed, trying to salvage what there was of her pride. Maybe he hadn't noticed how eager she had suddenly become. How much she wanted him.

Sure, as if that didn't happen to him all the time, she thought ruefully. What made her think that she was different from any of the others who wanted him? Women he could take or leave on whim.

"Saved by the bell," she murmured.

There was something sad in her voice, so sad that it twisted his heart, Hank thought. It made him want to sweep her into his arms and hold her until the sadness went away.

The impulse surprised him. He couldn't remember ever feeling protective of a woman before, as if he were directly tied to her feelings.

Lightly, he touched his lips to hers. "To be continued," he promised.

As she reached for the telephone, Fiona was certain her heart was going to pound right out of her chest.

"She is a gem," Collins said to Hank as he munched on one of the hors d'oeuvres that he had been consuming all evening. "I don't know where you found her, but I'm ready to make you a full partner for discovering this jewel." Fascinated, he looked down at what was left on his plate. "These crab cakes are fantastic. I must have eaten my weight in them and she keeps bringing in more. How does she do it?"

"She's living proof of the American edict. Old-fashioned hard work," Hank answered. "If you enjoy the food, why don't you tell her yourself, Jeff? I know she'd love to hear it."

Collins took another bite, savoring it every bit as much as his first one two hours ago. "I think I will."

Setting his empty plate down on a nearby surface, Jeffrey Collins plowed his considerable bulk through the gathering of clients and employees until he cornered Fiona.

"Young lady, I'd like a word with you."

Fiona stopped dead in her tracks, a feeling of déjà vu washing over her. Her father had always hauled her out on the carpet for one of his lengthy lectures with those very words. "Is anything wrong, Mr. Collins?"

"Wrong?" He laughed as he purloined another hors d'oeuvre from the tray she was holding. "It couldn't be more right. I don't know where you've been hiding, but I'm certainly happy that Hank brought you to our attention. You can be assured that there are a lot of people here who will want to avail themselves of your services. Just don't forget that we have first call on you." He made short work of the hors d'oeuvre then debated taking another, hesitating only because she was looking at him so intently. "My daughter's graduating college at the end of the summer. I'd like to have a little get-together for her. Pencil me in for the last Saturday in August, will you?" The debate went in his favor and he picked up another crab cake. "Love these things," he told her between bites as he walked away.

Though his compliments had been flattering, the conversation had left her puzzled. Fiona looked around for Hank. She saw him talking to another man and made her way over to him.

"Can I see you for a moment?" she asked.

Hank tried to read her expression. She didn't quite look like a woman who had been complimented. He thought of Collins's reputation. "What's the matter, did Collins come on to you?"

Fiona thought she heard something protective in his voice, but then decided that she'd just imagined it. "No, he just asked me to do some catering for him. Hank, he acted as if he didn't know anything about me. Wouldn't he at least know that I was a client with the firm?" Or was the firm so large that the man couldn't keep track of everyone associated with it?

He knew he should have told her earlier, but the right moment had never come up. It was here now, whether he liked it or not.

"Well," he began, "you're not exactly the firm's client. You're mine. Exclusively."

8

The words refused to compute. Fiona stared at Hank. The rest of the guests at the party faded into the background. "What does that mean exactly, 'yours exclusively'?"

Hank chose his words carefully. There was a certain look in her eyes he couldn't quite read. But twisters came in all sizes and shapes. He knew better than to run headlong into one.

"It means that when I signed on with Collins Walker, in addition to heading my own department and dealing with a number of major accounts, I had a clause put into my contract allowing me to take on a small account of my own if I saw some sort of merit in it." It had been the first step to eventually setting up his own firm, something he knew was destined to be in his future. And he saw so much merit in hers, he thought. "One that wouldn't be a threat to any of the accounts that Collins Walker already handles. That also means I get to use some of the firm's connections and their facilities at corporate rates. In exchange, should what I've taken on—on my own time," he emphasized, since this in no way was allowed to cut into company time, "prove, somewhere down the line to grow into a large account, I bring it into the fold."

He studied her face, waiting to see her reaction. So far, he couldn't read her expression. Maybe that was a good sign. "You might say that this is sort of like an orphan program."

The words penetrated immediately.

"And I'm the orphan."

He'd known he'd used the wrong term the minute it was out of his mouth. Hank tried to apply a little damage control, but he had the uneasy feeling that it might be too late.

"No, you're the account with potential that doesn't have the money to finance a large-sale advertising campaign." He could see she was far from convinced. Drawing on his salesmanship, Hank made another stab at making this palatable to her. "If I were a lawyer, this would be like taking a case pro bono."

Fiona knew exactly what that meant. And exactly how she felt about it. There was no way she was going to accept this. "Charity?"

They could bandy euphemisms back and forth all night. It still didn't change the bottom line. The bottom line was that she didn't have the kind of money that was needed to accomplish what she needed done. Not yet, anyway. But he wanted to help her. If not for Fiona, he might not have this job. Besides, he believed that everyone should do something that made them feel good about themselves once in a while. Helping her made him feel good about himself. Made him feel good, period.

"Don't get your pride up, Fiona. The charitable act being performed is by you to me."

He had to think she was really gullible. "And just how am I doing that?"

"By letting me get a foot in the door at the right time. I wasn't just whistling in the wind the other day. You are going to be big, lady. Real big. You just need the right kind of management."

Fiona felt herself weakening, but she wasn't completely convinced yet. It wasn't that she didn't believe in herself. If she hadn't, she wouldn't have gotten this far. It was just that she didn't quite see herself growing to such huge proportions.

"So you said."

"My dear, what are these delightful little things called?"

Fiona turned to see an older, mature-figured woman standing behind her. The woman was holding one of the miniature tarts she had slavishly made early this morning, improving on a recipe Mavis had once given her.

"Basically, it's pecan pie," Fiona replied.

The woman turned the tiny pie plate around on her plate with the edge of her fork. It resembled something that might be served to an elf and clearly delighted her. "Do you sell these?"

Fiona shook her head. "No."

"Not yet," Hank corrected as he intervened. He placed himself between Fiona and the woman he recognized as the owner of The High Life, a newly established restaurant that was becoming the latest trendy place to eat.

"'Yet'?" Fiona echoed. She looked at him quizzically. What was he talking about?

"But it's one of the things on the drawing board, Ms. Gentry." With an engaging smile tossed in the older woman's direction, Hank ushered Fiona off. He wanted to talk to her alone.

Alice Gentry had just enough time to take a crab cake from Fiona's tray before she was out of reach. The last Hank saw of the woman, her eyes were fluttering shut in gastronomic ecstasy.

He was sitting on a gold mine, he thought.

He was going too fast for her. "What things, what drawing board?" Fiona wanted to know. And there was one question standing head and shoulders above all the other questions she had. "And why didn't you tell me that you were doing all this on your own and not through the company?"

"Because of the expression on your face when you thought that this was some convoluted act of charity. Stick with me, lady," he said, slipping his arm around her shoulders, "and things are going to start happening for you."

Fiona tried not to let herself sink into the crook of his arm, though she was sorely tempted to. She had a feeling that things were already happening. The problem was, they had different spins on what they meant by "things."

* * *

"I don't think I can do this."

Fiona bit her lower lip uncertainly as she looked at the cameraman setting up on the small set. Hank had brought her here just ten minutes ago and introduced her to Tony Kiriakis. "The best TV commercial cameraman in the business," according to him. She wouldn't have known the man from Adam, but she trusted Hank.

Maybe a little too much. Her hand went to her stomach, which threatened to roll right up to her mouth.

The set she was on was equally divided to portray a living room and a large ballroom. It didn't matter what it was divided into, she was no actress. What did she know about delivering lines?

"Sure you can." As he spoke, Hank began to massage her shoulders. His heart went out to her. Her shoulders couldn't have been stiffer than if she'd been smuggling wooden coat hangers. But he knew she could do this. She would be a perfect pitchwoman if he could just get her to believe it. "The homey touch is in. Just look into the camera, say the words I wrote for you and you'll be just fine."

What was she doing here? her mind cried. She must have been crazy to let him talk her into this. But somehow the word "no" just didn't seem to materialize when she was around him.

"Easy for you to say," she murmured ruefully, "your palms don't feel like mini waterfalls."

Abandoning her shoulders, he moved in front of her and took her hands into his. Very slowly, his eyes on hers, he raised her hands to his lips. He kissed first one, then the other. "Better?"

"Oh, yes, much." There was a touch of desperate sarcasm in her voice, but she didn't pull her hands away. "Now my stomach's in an even bigger knot."

He laughed, moving behind her again. He seemed determined to make her fall apart, she thought as he resumed kneading her shoulders. This was not helping any. The slightest pressure from his hands sent shock waves all through her body.

She tried to turn around, but he held her firmly in place. "Now what are you doing?"

"Trying to get the tension out of your shoulders," Hank answered mildly. "This is just a thirty-second spot on a local channel." It was all he could arrange, between the check he'd finally accepted from her and some money of his own that he'd put in. He'd gotten both the studio space and Tony at cost as it was.

She saw the cameraman looking her way. Her stomach changed direction and dropped fifteen feet. "I suppose hoping no one sees it is self-defeating."

He laughed. "Very."

She pressed her lips together. Try as she might, she couldn't find anything positive to focus on. She was going through hell and there was probably going to be nothing gained by this. Why couldn't she convince Hank that the verbal referrals after the Collins Walker dinner were enough?

Fiona glanced over her shoulder at him. "Aren't cameras supposed to accent all your bad features?"

With a deliberate motion, he turned her head forward again. Some of the tension was actually beginning to leave her shoulders, though he doubted he could actually make her relax. "You don't have any bad features."

The short laugh was disparaging. "You're getting me mixed up with you."

"There you go again," Hank lamented, "flirting with me when I can't do anything about it." The only way to make her act natural, he thought, was to distract her. He bent close to her face, bringing his mouth to her ear. "Why don't we go somewhere private after this is over and get something to eat?"

She struggled not to shiver as his breath skimmed along her cheek. "A restaurant?"

"Actually," he whispered, lightly kissing her ear, "I was thinking more along the lines of your place."

The man had no idea what he was doing to her, she thought.

"All right." She barely managed to get the words out. "If you want."

He turned her around to face him. The teasing look had left his eyes. "I want."

The words seemed to vibrate in her chest. Fiona had to remind herself to breathe. Collapsing at his feet like a limp rag doll would ruin everything.

"Can we get on with this?" Tony called over to them. "I know that I'm not Steven Spielberg, but I do have a life, mundane though it is at times, and I'd really like to go home to it before I have to be back here again tomorrow."

"Sorry, Tony, we're almost ready." Hank looked

at Fiona, wanting to give her as much time as she needed. He lowered his voice. "Aren't we?"

She didn't want to disappoint him. After all, Hank was going out on a limb for her. Fiona was sure the check she'd given him didn't begin to cover all this. Thanks to conversations with her brother-in-law, she knew a little something about production costs. But not wanting to disappoint Hank wasn't enough. She still felt as if she was going to come off like a talking wooden stick.

Fiona hesitated. "I don't know."

"Pretend you're only talking to me," he coaxed, leading her over to the set. "Just to me."

Oh, yeah, like that was going to help calm her down, she thought.

But she had to admit that there was something endearing about the way he was coaching her.

"Hey, we're not doing *Gone With the Wind* here." Tony beckoned Fiona toward her first mark on the floor. "It's a thirty-second spot. You're in, you're out. Nothing to it." He went behind his camera, then looked out at her one last time. "Ready?"

Fiona took a deep breath. Her eyes darted to Hank. He gave her the high sign.

"Ready." As she would ever be, Fiona thought.

It turned out to be amazingly painless.

"Fastest shoot I ever did." Pleased, Tony looked at Fiona over the tops of his half-glasses. "The camera loves you, honey." He carefully shut the camera down. "You ever think of doing commercials professionally? 'Cause if you do, I've got this cousin who's got this agency—''

She exchanged looks with Hank. He wasn't laughing. Had they all lost their minds?

"Commercial work? Me? You're kidding, right?" She looked at Hank again. This time he was smiling. Suspicions immediately took hold. "Did you put him up to this?"

"All pretty boy here did was ask me to shoot this for him for an obscenely small amount of money. You've got that homespun, trustworthy look." Tony laughed as he came forward to join them. "Hell, I'd buy a used car from you."

Now that it was all over, she felt a great deal better. She might even look back at it as a fun experience, once her stomach stopped flipping over.

"Thanks, I'll remember that when my van gives out."

"Funny." Tony signaled to someone in the rear and the lights went down. The stage, so bright and friendly a moment ago, took on a dark, lonely look. "Well, I've gotta go home and do my husbandly duty." He chuckled under his breath as he looked from Fiona to Hank. "Woman can't keep her hands off me the minute I walk in the door."

"Newlyweds?" she guessed, though Tony Kiriakis didn't strike her as being the newlywed type. He was at least in his late forties and rather shopworn-looking.

Tony shook his head. "Going on ten years," he admitted proudly, then added, "If I last." He looked at her, an idea appearing to occur to him. "Maybe we'll have a celebration when we get there. Got one of your cards handy?"

The question caught her off guard. "Sure." She quickly took one out of her purse.

Tony examined the stick figure in the lefthand corner. "Cute. Doesn't look a thing like you." He glanced down. "Except for the shoes." He pocketed the card, then nodded at the tape in his hand. "I'll get this back to you tomorrow afternoon," he told Hank. "Good enough?"

"Absolutely."

With that agreed on, the cameraman took his leave, hurrying out the back way. Hank and Fiona made their way out through the front door.

They heard it a second before Hank opened the door. Thunder, echoing like a belated drumroll.

That couldn't be what he thought it was. Holding his breath, Hank pushed the door open. Sheets of rain were pouring out of the sky. The parking lot looked almost submerged.

It was his first experience with what natives liked to call liquid California sunshine. Hank stepped back. "Hey, I thought that rain was outlawed here, except for the winter months."

She laughed. Fiona had always loved the rain and the sound of thunder had never frightened her, even as a small child. She'd thought of it as angels letting everyone know they were still there.

She looked up to see if there was any lightning, but the sky remained dark.

"Sometimes the weatherman messes up." Fiona extended her hand, letting the rain fall on her bare arm.

Hank saw that it showed no signs of letting up. At this rate, they could be standing here all night. It was only several yards to the car, but they'd be drenched by the time they reached it.

"Why don't you stay here and I'll bring the car around?" Hank offered.

There was no way she intended to remain behind. "No, let's just make a run for it together." She saw the dubious expression on his face. "Don't worry, I won't melt. I'm not made of sugar."

He had a different opinion. To him, she was pure sugar—with just enough spice to make it interesting. But before he could say anything, Fiona had taken his hand and was pulling him to the lot.

In the short time they had been in the studio, puddles had formed everywhere. Rainwater slipped into her shoes, assaulting her legs from above and below.

By the time she reached the car, she was entirely soaked, as was he. Fiona didn't seem to care a damn about the fact that her clothes and her hair were plastered to her body.

If he didn't know any better, Hank thought, getting his keys out, she looked as if she was enjoying this. He quickly opened her side of the car, then hurried to the driver's side. Rain followed him in before he had a chance to shut the door.

"Wow," Fiona gasped, laughing. Scrubbing her hands over her face, she sent drops flying. "Sorry," she laughed when she realized she'd gotten some on him. As for herself, there wasn't a single part of her that wasn't sopping wet.

"What's a little extra rain?" He felt just the way he had felt as a kid, after hopping through puddles. "Hey, I offered to spare you," Hank reminded her as he started the car.

His silent prayer was answered and the engine turned over. Though a gorgeous thing to look at, his vintage car became somewhat unreliable when faced with conditions that weren't perfect.

Not unlike, Hank thought, a lot of women he knew. But not the one in his car.

She was dragging her fingers through her hair, chasing away some of the moisture. Her normally riotous hair clung to her scalp.

"Rain's good for the vegetation. Heaven knows we get little enough of it as it is." The last two winters had been particularly dry. At times, she wondered how anything grew at all.

When he didn't answer, Fiona glanced in his direction. The street lamps they drove past illuminated his profile. Water was dripping from his chin and the ends of his hair. Just looking at him made her heart ache. She longed to brush the raindrops from his hair. Fiona curled her fingers into her palms.

Very carefully, Hank picked his way out of the lot. The windshield wipers slapped against his window like a man trying to keep himself warm. Visibility was miserable. "Most women I know don't like getting washed away in a flash flood."

She laughed at the description. "You think this is bad—'you ain't seen nothing yet.' Wait until the real rainy season," she warned. "In a bad year—" and they were predicting a bad year "—it feels as if Southern California is just going to wash away."

Terrific. "I'm looking forward to it," Hank muttered, his eyes peeled for the exit.

The sudden deluge had driven most of the late-night traffic off the road. Despite poor visibility, they made it to her house in relatively good time, especially considering that it was a Friday night.

When he pulled up in her driveway, she debated asking him in. The shoot and the rain had made her slightly euphoric, but she supposed there was no sense in being foolhardy.

Fiona opened the door just a crack, enough to send tiny raindrops scurrying into the interior of the car. "Maybe you'd better go on home. You don't want to catch cold."

She wasn't getting rid of him that easily, Hank thought. They had gotten together after-hours for two solid weeks now, hashed ideas out and set a couple into motion, including this commercial. In all that time, he'd found himself liking Fiona and her slightly quirky behavior more and more. He wanted to find out just how much more.

"It takes more than getting caught in a little drizzle to get me sick," he told her. "I've milked cows in a blizzard."

"Now there's something I could probably live out

my life without experiencing.'' Bracing herself, she swung her door open all the way.

''Don't knock it till you try it,'' he countered. At the time he'd hated it, but the childhood he'd had had gone a long way in making him the man he was now. Prepared for almost anything.

His shoulders hunched against the rain, he followed her to the front door. She fumbled with the key.

Fiona turned the key in the lock, then struggled to retrieve it. The key wouldn't budge. Fiona gritted her teeth. ''It's stuck.''

''Here, let me try.'' It took several twists of the wrist before the key finally came out. ''You need to oil that thing.''

Fiona closed the door behind him. She saw her reflection in the hall mirror. A drowned cat probably had a better hairstyle, she thought, but right now she felt too good to care.

''So I keep telling myself. But by the time I walk into the kitchen where I keep the WD-40, I forget.'' She sighed, unrepentant. ''There's just so much to do.''

He'd been raised in that kind of atmosphere, the kind that dictated that you did a thing when you thought of it or else it would get buried in the shuffle.

''No time like the present.'' He dragged his hand through his hair. Drops scattered all around his head. ''Where do you keep the container?''

''Under the sink.'' She began to follow him. ''But you don't have to—''

He had already retrieved it and was on his way back. "Hey, I like being handy. Soothe my ego and let me play macho."

She took the small can from him when he was finished. "You don't have to play at it. You are." She set the can aside, feeling oddly serene. Maybe it was the rain. It always made her feel so cozy. "So, what would you like?"

His mouth curved as he turned to look at her. "Something cold and wet."

Her eyes never left his face. "Right now, that description could fit me."

Hank took her hand, moving closer. "I know."

Though tiny nerve endings finally came to life, Fiona couldn't have moved unless the whole foundation of the house had begun to slide. "You don't want to eat, do you?"

Very slowly, he moved his head from side to side, his eyes caressing her face. "Not particularly."

Could he hear her heart hammering? Or were those her knees making that noise? "What do you want?"

"You."

He whispered it so softly, she was afraid she was going to cry. And that he would misunderstand her tears. "You're going to be disappointed."

"Shh." He placed his finger to her lips. He wanted no protests, no disclaimers. He only wanted her. "Let me be the judge of that."

Moved by instincts, by an overwhelming need to connect, Fiona pressed her lips to the finger he held against them. She saw a strange look enter his eyes.

A look that was equal parts tender and passionate and left her instantly weak.

Hank dropped his finger, replacing it with his lips as he pulled her even closer to him. His mouth covered hers as desire, intense and demanding, rapped urgent knuckles at the walls of his restraint.

He had no more restraint. What he had was an overwhelming need to make love to this woman who intrigued him so.

Fiona's head began to spin again. Just for now, just for this evening, she would delude herself. She would pretend that she was just as beautiful as Bridgette, as beautiful as the women who passed through Hank's life had to be.

And just for now, she would pretend that this was not a one-time thing, but something that was the beginning of forever.

The way she fervently wished it was.

Hank hardly recognized her. She seemed to transform in his arms. The timid, shy girl was gone, replaced by a woman whose kisses had turned urgent. Whose desire seemed to be as towering as his own.

He had no idea he could become so aroused, so excited.

She was a revelation.

She was an experience. As he was drawn deep into the distinctly different layers of making love with her, it somehow brought him closer to himself than he had ever been. In making love with Fiona, from the most minute contact, he began to feel things he'd never felt before. Tastes, sounds, sensations, all new, all swirled around him, crowding his senses, his mind. Opening them like windows that had been left shut for too long.

She smelled of spring wildflowers, like the ones he remembered in his mother's kitchen. Like new-mown hay when it first sat in the fields, waiting to be gathered.

She smelled of home, he realized somewhere in the recesses of his mind as he covered her body with a rush of urgent kisses.

It was a strange feeling for a man his age to suddenly realize that he had left home looking for a piece of it in this corner of the world.

It was stranger still to realize that he had found it within a woman whose image he had doodled on the side of his yellow pad.

9

The scent of wildflowers drifted to him a moment before he woke up.

Wildflowers.

Fiona.

Hank reached for her as he slowly opened his eyes, only to discover that he was reaching for air. Fiona wasn't there.

Moving his hand over where she had slept, he found that her side of the bed was cool. She'd been gone for a while.

Hank looked at his watch. It was just barely seven o'clock. Way too early to be up on a Saturday, especially since they hadn't gotten all that much sleep last night.

Disappointment nibbled at him. He had envisioned a long, decadent morning where they would make slow love to each other before either set foot on the floor.

Obviously, they'd had different plans for the start of their day.

With a reluctant sigh, Hank got up and looked around for his jeans. He wasn't sure where he had tossed them. His mind hadn't been on his jeans at the time. Last night was a haze that was still clinging to his mind as well as his body.

Several minutes later he finally found them under the bed.

Hank smiled to himself as he pulled them on, the memory of Fiona settling warmly over his thoughts. She had been incredible once they had cracked open the door to this unexpected side of her.

Well, maybe not so unexpected, he mused, running his hands through his hair in lieu of combing it. He'd had a feeling, looking into her eyes that very first time, that there was passion there, just beneath the surface. But then, he'd also figured that she would be here this morning when he woke up, so he could hold her and remember last night.

And do it all over again.

He figured he was batting five hundred. Not bad for his first time at bat in this particular game.

Except that it didn't quite feel like a game to him. It felt like something...

Something more.

The adage about recognizing something only when he finally came across it whispered along his mind. His grandfather had told him that. It had been one of the few conversations he'd ever had with the solemn old man. Hank remembered every detail. You always remembered when it came to the most important moments in your life.

Just as he remembered every detail of last night.

Hank looked around for his shirt, then remembered

that it was in the living room. Was she in the living room, as well? He went to find out.

The yelp was strictly involuntary as he felt Velcro wrap herself around his leg, one claw sinking into his bare foot just as he crossed the threshold into the living room. A crash from the kitchen came in response to his cry. It sounded as if something had broken.

When he hobbled into the kitchen with Velcro still firmly attached to the lower part of his leg, Hank saw Fiona on her knees, picking up the pieces of what had once been a blue mixing bowl. What looked like pancake batter pooled around the pieces. There was a flash of embarrassment in the quick glance she spared him before looking down again.

Moving awkwardly because of the temporary ornament he was sporting, Hank joined her.

"Velcro, scat!" Fiona ordered. Her voice was far more forceful than anything Hank had heard from her before. Velcro obviously felt the same way because she scurried off.

Hank gingerly picked up the blue and white pieces. "I missed you in bed this morning."

Fiona had no idea that this was going to feel so awkward. She had no experience with waking up with a man in her bed. "Um, I had to get up."

He dumped the pieces into the trash. "Catering a party today?"

It would have been easy just to say yes and hide behind that. But she didn't want to end what had happened last night with a lie.

"No."

"But cooking relaxes you," Hank remembered. The way she was avoiding looking at him told him he was right before she said a word.

"Yes."

She was piling the pieces on top of one another in her hand. He took them from her and threw them out. Carefully dusting off her palm, he took her hand in his and rose to his feet, pulling her up with him.

She was standing before him, no makeup, her hair still tousled, looking as delectable as any woman he had ever seen. Seeing no reason to resist, Hank took her into his arms.

"I know other ways that might get you to that same goal. And we could do them together."

Being with him definitely did *not* relax her, Fiona realized. Besides, she didn't want him to feel as if he owed it to her. "You don't have to."

"Have to?" He studied her face, appearing confused. "That's a strange way to put it. Did any of the lovemaking last night seem forced to you in any way?" As he spoke, he toyed with the outline of her ear.

She felt herself growing warm, unable to concentrate. Shivers were beginning to dance along her spine. "No, last night was wonderful." It was more than that. "Beautiful," she corrected.

"Then what's the problem?" Hank couldn't understand why she was acting as if she were nervous again.

"There isn't a problem." How could she explain

this to him without humiliating herself? Fiona wondered. "I'd just thought that…now that you're awake…you'd just want to slip out and go home."

She felt as if she was tripping over every word. Why couldn't he have just gone and left her with her memory instead of putting her through this?

"'Now that I'm awake,'" Hank repeated, trying to understand just what it was she was attempting to tell him. "Did I act as if I were asleep last night?"

"No, but last night was last night and today is…well, today."

Now he was really confused. "That's a very profound statement and I'm sure someone's going to want to add it to their collection of proverbs, but what the hell are you saying?"

She raised her chin defensively. "That you don't have to feel obligated to me. That I know that you just want to go home now that it's done."

She thought it was a one-night stand, he realized. Hank didn't know whether to be insulted or to apologize if he'd somehow given her the impression that he was using her for his own end.

"'Obligated'? I don't feel obligated to you. I think you've got a slightly distorted picture here and you need to adjust your antenna, lady. I don't want to go home, and what I feel, Fiona, is hungry."

"I can—" She turned toward the refrigerator, but he caught her hand, stopping her.

"Not that kind of hungry," he told her, tugging her back to him. He nipped her lower lip and felt her yielding. Excitement roared through his veins with a speed that astounded him. "That kind," he breathed.

He still wanted her, Fiona realized. Despite the fact that they had made love half the night, he wanted her. A tenderness tugged at her heart. "Are you sure?"

He cupped her face in his hands, kissing her again. "I'm sure."

She fought to keep her mind from sinking into the paradise he was opening up. "But we just made love last night."

"Did we?" he murmured. He kissed each one of her eyelids as they fluttered seductively shut before him. "Oh, right. Well, since my memory's so poor, we'll just have to do it again until it sticks." Tiny kisses feathered along her mouth, bit by bit. "Or until I'm dead, whichever comes first." He grinned at her as he looked into her face. "Personally, since I'm in pretty good health, I'm hoping the end is a very long time off."

"But—"

He kissed away her protest until she was almost numb, then said, "Now, we can stand here and talk all you want. And I surely don't mind talking to you, but I thought that maybe we could get a little more comfortable while we did it. Like in your bed."

She slipped her hand into his. "All right."

Hank glanced over his shoulder at the stove just before he led her out of the kitchen. "Got anything going that might boil over?"

"Only me."

As he looked down at her face, something elusive slipped its hold on him. "Perfect."

It was a dream. A big, beautiful dream. And she knew it. Any second now she was going to wake up and discover that these past few weeks she'd spent with him had all been just part of a misty memory, no different than the very first dream she'd had of him.

It was just lasting longer, that was all.

She wanted it to last longer still. She wanted, very simply, for it to last forever.

Fat chance.

Fiona looked at him, her heart all but twisting in her breast. They'd worked late last night. He'd pretended that he was too tired to take her home, then negated that by making love with her. Over and over again.

The lovemaking had been incredibly magnificent, the kind she wouldn't have even been able to imagine if not for him. He'd been by turns tender, passionate, then gentle again. He'd driven her out of her mind, showing her how very empty her existence had been before him.

And how very empty it was going to be once he tired of her.

He was lying beside her, facedown on his pillow, his hair messy and in his eyes. Or it would have been, had his eyes been open. Fiona resisted the impulse to touch him, to stroke his hair, to whisper just how much she cared about him.

How much, she realized, she loved him.

With slow, tiny movements, she inched her way to the edge of the bed. She wanted to get up without waking him. She knew how much he liked coffee first thing in the morning. The coffeemaker he had had outlived its usefulness. It certainly couldn't make the kind of coffee she could.

Fiona smiled to herself, one foot touching the floor. She wanted to spoil Hank, to somehow make him feel that if she wasn't in his life, he'd feel as if something irreplaceable was missing. Barring that, she wanted to hold on to him with both hands so that he'd never fade from her life.

Big mistake.

Hold something too tightly and it would just break away. She knew that. All she could do was pray that he'd remain in her life a little longer.

Gaining the floor with both feet, Fiona began to slip from the bed, only to feel her wrist being caught. Surprised, she turned to see Hank looking at her, his face still communing with his pillow. The one eye she saw was staring at her blearily.

"Where are you going?" The words were muffled against his pillow.

Very carefully, she peeled his fingers back from her wrist. He looked to be still half asleep. "To make you some coffee."

"Coffee." The word left his lips, a prayer onto itself. He sighed, as if he'd just sighted the gates of heaven. "Have I told you that I love you?"

Her heart slammed against her chest, a tennis ball lobbed against a wall by an overly muscled pro.

He had said he loved her.

With supreme effort, Fiona banked down her emotions, her desire to echo the words back to him. He didn't mean that. It was the sleep talking, nothing more. Once he was awake, he wouldn't even remember saying it.

"No," she whispered, "you haven't."

"Well," he muttered into the pillow, "I do."

Fiona squared her shoulders, trying very hard not to let herself get carried away. "I'll go make coffee."

"Angel." The pronouncement faded into the pillow. He was asleep again.

For just a moment she lingered at the foot of the bed, lingering, too, over the scene. "If I were an angel, I'd move heaven and earth to make this last," she said softly, too softly for him to hear.

But she wasn't an angel; all she could do was make him coffee.

Opening the bureau drawer, Fiona selected one of his T-shirts and dragged it on. Sufficiently covered, she padded out to the kitchen.

She hadn't thought she'd wind up here like this last night. He'd originally come to her place to work, but then he'd remembered that her commercial was airing just before the ten o'clock news. Since it was the first time, he wanted her to see it on a big-screen television. His. When the commercial had come on, she'd been almost too embarrassed to watch, peering instead through the crack between her hands as she held them up over her face. It had been too painful for her to endure.

Fiona took the can of imported coffee she had given him as a small gift from the refrigerator door. Hank had been exceedingly complimentary once the program resumed. Complimentary and so tender toward her that she had all but melted into his arms.

Fiona took a pot, filled it with water and placed it on the front burner. Blue flame encircled its bottom. Every time she was around the man, her body composition changed from solid to liquid. If this kept up, the man was going to have to carry her around in one of those plastic sandwich bags.

As if he'd want to.

There was no deluding herself, no matter how much she would have wanted to. Her father, for all his thoughtless, hurtful remarks, had succeeded in one thing. He'd made her a realist. She had made herself an optimist, but only after much trying and even then, the optimism was firmly grounded in reality.

As it was now.

What she had at this moment was more wonderful than anything she could have ever imagined for herself, but wonderful or not, it was going to end.

It had already gone on far longer than she would have thought it would. Her luck was holding out an inordinate amount of time. But it was, she knew, just a matter of when, not if.

She heard the water boiling. Fiona poured it

through the old-fashioned percolator it had taken her months to find. She'd brought it with her last night for the sole purpose of giving him a "decent" cup of coffee, hoping it would take his mind off the commercial. He'd used the cup to toast her with.

The doorbell rang, startling her. She looked over her shoulder toward the bedroom. "Hank, are you expecting anyone?" she called.

Instead of a response, she heard the sound of water being turned on. He was taking a shower. She struggled with the impulse to join him. The doorbell rang again.

Hesitating, she finally walked over to the door. Hank had installed a small security camera when he saw that the peephole yielded too distorted a view of whoever was ringing the bell.

Fiona looked at the black-and-white monitor and saw a statuesque woman on the doorstep. She was leaning against his bell.

"C'mon, Hank, open up the damn door," the woman called, looking straight into the security camera. "I know you're in there. I didn't come all this way just to talk to you through a door."

Well, whoever the woman was, she obviously knew him well enough to yell at him. Bracing herself, Fiona unlocked the front door.

Rather than enter, the woman, a vivacious-looking blonde dressed in a black leather jacket and black jeans, looked her up and down in surprise. Fiona noticed a motorcycle helmet tucked under her arm.

A full head taller than Fiona, the woman smiled slightly, as if sharing some joke with herself.

After a beat, she decided to share the joke with Fiona. "I came because I thought he might be lonely." She sauntered in, shaking her head. "I should have known better." The blonde turned to face her. Fiona thought she saw amusement in her eyes. "I'll say this for him, Hank doesn't waste any time, does he?"

Was this an ex-lover? Or maybe a current one she didn't know about? A sinking feeling hit the pit of Fiona's stomach.

Either way, the woman was far more in keeping with the kind of woman Fiona envisioned Hank with. Tall, slender, blond, with a face that would have been called beautiful even if it were covered with mud.

Bridgette's kind of face, Fiona thought. But not hers.

"So, where are you keeping him?" the woman quipped. She looked around the room, as if expecting Hank to materialize out of the walls.

"He's in the shower." Fiona bit her lower lip. That sounded much too intimate. "I mean—" She took a deep breath, forcing herself to sound calm. "There's some coffee in the kitchen, would you like some?"

The blonde's eyes lit up. "Right now, sugar, I would kill for some coffee." She threw off her jacket, dropping it and the helmet onto the nearest chair. She seemed far more at home here than Fiona was.

"Help yourself." Fiona gestured toward the percolator with as much dignity as she could muster. "I have to be going." She hurried from the room.

"Hey, don't run off on my account," the woman called after her.

"I'm not," Fiona answered, not sure if the woman heard her. It didn't matter.

She wasn't leaving on the other woman's account, she was leaving on her own account, Fiona thought, hurrying into her clothes. She kept one eye on the door, praying Hank wouldn't come out until she was finished and gone.

What an idiot she'd been, thinking that she could make this work. The woman in the kitchen was the sort of woman who belonged with Hank, not her. A beautiful woman who was comfortable with herself, comfortable in any environment she found herself in.

Not like her, Fiona thought ruefully. She pushed her hands through her shirt, a shirt that was missing a button because Hank had been so eager to touch her.

Her heart tightened in her chest.

All she wanted to do was get back to where she belonged. In her kitchen, creating dishes to make people happy. Not deluding herself that she could accomplish the same thing without a stove.

Made it, she thought, grabbing her shoes and her purse. Hank was still in the shower.

"Great coffee," the blonde told her, catching a glimpse of Fiona as she quickly made her way to the front door. "Want me to say anything to Hank for you?"

Fiona paused only for a moment. "Just tell him…tell him now that the main event is here, the warm-up act went home."

The woman frowned as the front door closed. Strange little thing, she mused. For a minute there, she had thought that Hank's taste had definitely improved, but maybe that wasn't the case.

Finishing her coffee, she debated taking another cup, then decided against it. She rinsed out her cup and placed it on the side of the sink.

A movement behind her caught her attention. When she turned to see Hank walking into the kitchen, wearing nothing but a towel precariously knotted at his waist, Morgan Cutler smiled broadly.

"Is this what the well-dressed hunk is wearing these days in California? Don't make any sudden moves, brother dear, or I'll get to see just how much you've filled out since we all went skinny-dipping at the creek when we were kids."

Hank stopped dead. His hand immediately went to the knot to make certain it was secure. "What are you doing here?"

"Admiring the view," Morgan answered tongue-in-cheek. "Really, Hank, is that any way to greet your baby sister? And after I rode all the way down here to see you, too." Crossing to him, Morgan brushed his cheek with her lips.

"You know I'm glad to see you." He looked around. He could smell the coffee, but there wasn't any sign of the woman who had prepared it. Where the hell had she gotten to? "Have you seen Fiona?"

"Fiona," Morgan repeated. She liked the way the name wrapped around her tongue. It sounded a lot more melodic to her than her own did, although she'd always felt Morgan suited her just fine. "That would be the cute little thing wearing one of your old T-shirts?"

"Yes," he answered impatiently. "Where is she?"

Morgan made herself comfortable at the counter, deciding that yes, she would have another cup of coffee. Something told her she might need it. She took it black, like the ace of spades. "She left."

"Left?" he echoed. Hank strode back to her. "What did you say to her?"

"Nothing."

She batted her eyes at him, the soul of innocence. He didn't usually mind Morgan's teasing, but he wasn't in the mood for it right now. There was no reason for Fiona to have left without a word. Everything had been perfect last night.

"But she said something to me," Morgan volunteered.

"What?"

He bit off the word. Morgan had a feeling it was going to be her head next. The display of edginess was very unusual in her brother. Morgan began to study him a tad closer.

"She told me to tell you that the warm-up act was leaving now that the main event was here."

Warm-up act? What the hell was that supposed to mean? Had Fiona somehow gotten the crazy notion that Morgan was an old girlfriend?

The very thought chilled him. Hank grabbed Morgan's shoulder and turned her around to face him. "Did you tell her you were my sister?"

"Careful, another sudden move like that and you might catch cold where you can't afford to." She lifted her chin playfully, indicating that her eyes were riveted to his face. "I didn't have time to tell her anything. She was out of here before I fully realized that she was your latest conquest." Morgan smiled, her blue eyes crinkling. "I must say, you've finally hooked yourself up to someone who doesn't look like an airhead."

Annoyed, Hank poured himself a cup of coffee, laced it with milk and downed it quickly. He frowned. The cup rattled as he put it down on the counter. "The problem is, she doesn't seem to want to stay hooked."

Morgan stared at him, trying to see if he was serious. "To you? Hank, sugar, you're too young to have lost your touch."

He blew out a breath. Damn it, what did he have to do to convince Fiona that he was serious? That he wanted to build something between them? "I don't give a damn about my 'touch,' I just don't want to lose Fiona."

The playfulness left Morgan's eyes. Hank was the last of her brothers she'd have thought would be hit by Cupid. "This sounds serious."

He paused before going back to his room to put on some clothes. "Yeah, it is."

Admitting it out loud gelled it for him. And told him what he had to do next.

10

When he left the house, Hank fully expected to overtake Fiona walking toward the main drag outside the development.

But she was nowhere to be seen.

Just his luck, she'd probably managed to find a cab letting someone off in the development, he thought angrily. Taking a shortcut, he arrived at her block in time to see a blue and white car with a lit Taxi sign atop its roof turning away.

"Damn it, woman, why can't you stay put?" Hank muttered to himself.

He pulled up sharply in her driveway, narrowly avoiding her van. Hank was at the front door in five strides, punching his forefinger at her doorbell.

There was no answer.

"Fiona, open the door. I know you're in there." When she didn't comply immediately, he began knocking. Knocking quickly escalated into banging as his fist made contact with the wood.

Fiona jerked open the door. The expression on his face startled her, but she was good at holding her own in the face of anger. It was the dream of tenderness that made her fall apart.

She scowled at Hank. "You'll wake up the whole neighborhood."

He strode in, slamming the door behind him. It pained him to see her jump like that, but the pain in his gut was even worse.

"Right now, I don't much care if the whole damn neighborhood loses its beauty sleep or not." He was struggling to hold on to his temper. There was no reason for her to do this. He'd thought they'd gotten beyond this point. "Why the hell did you just run off like that?"

Fiona shrugged, looking away. "I figured you wanted to be alone."

She wasn't making any sense. "Alone?"

Did she have to spell it out for him? "With that gorgeous woman who showed up."

Hank realized he'd been right, she had run off because she thought Morgan was an old girlfriend. Even if Morgan had been an old girlfriend, that was no reason for Fiona to just take off like that.

"I'm sure Morgan would love the compliment, but why would I want to be alone with my sister?"

Fiona realized her mistake as soon as she heard the name. "Your sister?"

When the hell was she going to trust him? "My sister." Because he wanted to shake her, he shoved his hands into his pockets. "And if you hadn't run off like some scared jackrabbit with a coyote on her tail, you would have found that out."

Fiona took offense at the image, even though she knew she deserved it. Maybe she'd acted rashly, but mistaking Morgan for an old girlfriend only showed her how really foolish she'd been, hanging on to her dreams. Someday, maybe soon, an old girlfriend would show up. Or worse yet, a brand-new one. A man like Hank would never be hers.

Fiona drew herself up. "Maybe this is for the best."

His eyebrows furrowed until they formed a single, wavy light-brown line above his nose. Now what was she going on about? Hank wondered. He swore women should come with instruction manuals. But even if they did, with his luck, the manuals would probably be written in a foreign language.

"What 'best'? What 'this'? Fiona, what are you talking about?"

She was drawing on all the inner strength she had to say this without breaking down. "Look, we've had a wonderful time together—"

"Had?"

There was a dangerous note in his voice she'd never heard before.

Fiona pressed on. If she didn't get this out now, she never would. "Yes, had."

She wanted to pace, to twist her hands together, to somehow find a way to manage this horrible, un-settled feeling that was consuming her. But that would only make her seem like some nervous little twit and she didn't want his last memory of her to be that.

"I couldn't expect it to go on much longer, not in a place where every fifth woman that you trip over is some drop-dead gorgeous creature who wants to become a movie star."

His eyes were flinty, as if he didn't understand what she was saying. "I hadn't noticed that I've been tripping over women."

Frustrated, she threw her hands up. Didn't he know how hard this was for her? Didn't he appreciate the fact that she was giving him a graceful way out? "You know what I mean."

"No, I don't. I don't know what you mean at all." He crossed his arms before him, his eyes never leaving her face. "Explain it to me."

Somehow, she managed to steel herself off. She said it as simply as possible. "You're a very handsome man. You belong with a gorgeous woman."

It went over like a lead balloon. She didn't expect to see the anger that entered his eyes. "Is this some sort of convoluted reverse prejudice?" he demanded heatedly. "I'm good-looking, therefore I don't have brains?"

He was twisting things. She'd never meant to insult him. "No—"

He cut her off, too angry to listen.

"That's what it sounds like to me." Hank couldn't remember feeling this angry, except maybe when his grandfather had died. He hadn't been able to do anything about it then, either. "You're treating me as if all there is to me is vanity, as if I belong on top of one of your wedding cakes, next to an equally fake figure of a woman.''

Fiona placed her hand on his arm, trying to make him understand that what she was doing was for both their own good. She couldn't bear him looking at her someday and saying it was over, that he'd found someone he really cared about.

''No, that's not what I'm saying.''

But whether she realized it or not, that was exactly what she was saying, Hank thought. He shrugged her off. ''Do you think I'm stupid, Fiona? That all I want is someone who looks gorgeous on my arm?''

Fiona squared her shoulders. She was being adult about this and he was yelling at her as if she were a child. Yelling at her just the way her father had. ''No, I don't think you're stupid, but why shouldn't you want someone who's gorgeous?''

He turned the tables on her. ''Is that what you want? Is that why you're with me?'' he demanded. When she took a step back, he matched it until he had her up against a wall, both figuratively and literally. ''From everything you've said, you seem to think I belong in that category—good-looking, the kind of man who makes women's heads turn. Am I just a hood ornament for you?''

She stared at him, wide-eyed. How could he possibly think that she felt that way about him? ''No, it's not like that.''

He glared at her. Where there was smoke, there was fire. ''You wouldn't be saying it if it wasn't on your mind.''

Anger, hot and defensive, kicked in. ''Don't you raise your voice at me.''

Hank wanted to do more than raise it, he wanted to shout in her face until somehow she came to her senses. But her hotly voiced protest made him realize that neither one of them was willing to give an inch.

He blew out a breath, taking stock of himself. ''Sorry. Maybe we both need a little time off here.'' He backed away from her, surprised how far his anger would have taken him if he'd let it. ''Maybe things have been going too fast for both of us.'' They had been for him, he realized. He'd been thinking things about her that he'd never even considered before.

He was at the door before she could say anything.

''Sorry I disturbed your neighborhood.'' The door slammed, a final coda to the scene that had just taken place.

Fiona stood, staring at the closed door, feeling as if everything inside her was shattering. In the course of a few short minutes she'd somehow managed to bring about everything she'd hoped could be held off for just a little while longer.

She stood stock-still for a very long time before she began to cry.

''So call him,'' Bridgette urged, frustration mounting in her voice. Fiona seemed to be getting worse with each day that passed. It was like watching a flower die without being able to do anything about it. Except that this time, she was related to the flower.

"Fiona, for heaven's sake, if you love him, call him."

There was no "if" about it, Fiona silently conceded.

She'd thought of calling him. A hundred times she'd thought of it. Once or twice she'd even dialed all the numbers before putting the receiver down again.

"And do what? Grovel?" Fiona cried. She caught herself. Bridgette only meant well. She shouldn't be taking out her feelings on her. "Plead that he stay for just a little while longer?" she asked more evenly. "Then I'd have to go through this again when he decides that he's tired of me."

Bridgette had forced Fiona to go over the whole scene for her, bit by bit. She'd gleaned things that seemed to have escaped her usually more savvy sister.

"He didn't sound as if he were tired of you, just your damn insecurity." She took hold of Fiona's shoulders. "Fiona, get this through your head. You're not an ugly duckling, you never were."

Fiona shrugged Bridgette off. Helpful or not, lies had no place here. "Did you have the same childhood I did?"

Bridgette put her own interpretation on the question. She'd always been the favored one and she knew it. "No, but I was there. Yes, I was prettier than you, the classic kind of pretty that Dad, in his warped sense of priorities, expected."

They both knew what their father had been like,

what had made him tick. He was a first-rate real estate agent, a salesman down to the very bottom of his shoes. He was into appearances and gingerbread trimmings. They both knew that was why he had married their mother in the first place. Because she was the kind of woman he wanted on his arm: beautiful.

Bridgette had loved her father, but that did not change what he was. "He was a shallow, shallow man who was just into surface things and he never looked beyond that."

A bitter smile twisted Fiona's lips. "Beyond that," she repeated. "Right, that would be inner beauty."

Bridgette took offense of her own. It hadn't been all roses and lollipops on her end of it, either. "Hey, don't knock it. I was considered empty-headed. You were the smart one."

That hadn't counted for very much and they both knew it. "So if someone wanted their algebra homework done, they came to me. If they wanted to see a movie, or go to a party, or have a great time, they came to you." Bridgette had been the one with more dates than days of the week. Fiona had been the one who had sat home. And had her father rub her nose in it.

Bridgette lost her temper. "Stop it, Fiona. Take a good look at yourself. A real good look." She forcibly turned Fiona toward the hall mirror and made her look into it. "You were never anything but what you made yourself. Did you ever try to work with your looks? I was there with a slew of makeup—you wouldn't even put on lipstick," Bridgette reminded her angrily. She gestured at herself, at her face. "What I've got is fifty percent illusion. You're genuine." Why couldn't Fiona see that? Her voice softened. "And, with a little work, you would be so stunning, I would probably hate you."

A smile began to form, a genuine one. Fiona could never stay mad at Bridgette, even when they were younger. Bridgette had never flaunted her looks, or her boyfriends. It was just the way things were.

"You're just saying that."

Bridgette's expression matched hers. "About hating you, yeah. But the rest of it's true." Their eyes met in the mirror. "Just let me get my hands on your face for a little while and I'll show you just how gorgeous you could be."

Fiona had never cared for the idea of layers of makeup on her face. "No, I—"

Bridgette arched an eyebrow. "Chicken?" Not waiting for an answer, she began making clucking noises.

"Of course not."

Hands tucked under her armpits, Bridgette added a visual dimension as she continued clucking.

Fiona held up her hands, surrendering. "All right, Fairy Godmother, wave your wand. Let me see what you can do."

Bridgette was already reaching for her purse. "I left my wand in my other outfit, but I just so happen to have my makeup bag with me." She pushed Fiona down onto a chair and dropped her bag on the kitchen counter. "Sit and be amazed."

It didn't take long.

Finished, Bridgette stepped back to admire her handiwork. Rather than say anything, she gestured Fiona toward the mirror in the hall.

Fiona was almost afraid to look. Afraid that, after all of Bridgette's efforts, she wouldn't see a difference. But there was. A distinct yet subtle difference. She was, in Bridgette's words, amazed.

"Wow."

"That's what I say." Bridgette came up behind her. She'd been surprised herself to see just how beautiful Fiona actually looked "enhanced." "I feel a little like Dr. Frankenstein, awed at what I've created, but not really too sure if I want to take a chance and unleash you on the unsuspecting world."

Though impressed, Fiona wouldn't have gone as far as call herself beautiful. Words like that belonged to Bridgette and to their mother, not her. "It's not that much of a change."

Bridgette knew what she saw, knew, too, that Fiona was stubborn. She remained undaunted. "See, I win both ways, don't I?" Still behind Fiona, she leaned forward, bringing her face next to her sister's. "Bottom line is, it's what you have inside that counts, Fiona. And from what you've told me, Hank picked up on that. I think you owe him an apology."

Fiona shrugged, turning away from the mirror. "I don't think he'll talk to me. He hasn't called in over a week." She sighed, going over the tally. "One week, two days, five hours and twenty-six minutes."

Fiona had it bad, Bridgette thought. "Not that anyone's keeping track," she murmured wryly. "Maybe you really hurt his feelings."

Fiona had another take on the situation. She couldn't picture anyone pining over her. "And maybe he's consoling himself with someone else." She saw the protest rising to Bridgette's lips. "No matter what I look like on the outside, I can't throw myself at him."

Bridgette had had just about enough of this holding back nonsense. You didn't just let a man like Hank Cutler get away over a misunderstanding. "How about if I threw you at him?"

Fiona gave her a warning look. "Bridgette, don't you dare do anything."

"You can be a very infuriating person, you know that?"

Fiona shrugged. "Stubbornness is my best feature, don't you know that?"

Bridgette's expression softened. She touched Fiona's cheek. "No, your heart is. Don't you know that?"

"Thanks." But she still didn't want Bridgette interfering. "'Member what Grandma used to say? If something was meant to be, it would be?"

They both knew what their grandmother had been like. Blending in with the times, she pretended to be meek and mild. But she'd never fooled the women in the family. "Yes, but that was also her facade.

She was a conniver, remember?'' Bridgette hooked her arm through Fiona's. ''C'mon, I feel a shopping spree coming on.''

For once, Fiona had no work planned for the afternoon. Unwilling to be alone with her thoughts, she offered no resistance to the suggestion.

But just as they reached the door, the fax machine perched on the kitchen counter came to life. Fiona looked at it over her shoulder, hesitating.

Bridgette was not about to give up a shopping trip because of some wayward piece of paper. ''If it's business, it'll keep until we get back,'' she coaxed.

Work was better for her than the mall any day. Fiona went back to the kitchen. ''I'm not doing *that* well yet, Bridgette. Every potential client is important.''

The machine had spit the paper out onto the floor. She picked it up just as another was peeking out of the opening, snaking its way out.

Resigned, Bridgette walked into the kitchen. ''So, is it for another wedding?''

Fiona stared at the paper in her hand, rereading it. ''No.''

There was an odd expression on her sister's face. Curious, Bridgette pressed, ''Anniversary?''

''No. It's a proposal.'' Fiona looked up. She was afraid to let herself believe that what she'd read was on the level. ''From Hank.'' She held up the page for Bridgette to look at. All it said was, ''Marry me. Hank.'' Fiona bit her lower lip. ''Think he sent it to the wrong number again?''

About to throw her arms around Fiona in congratulations, Bridgette stopped dead. How could she even suggest that?

"No, and if you do, you're about to get the beating of your life." Bridgette looked down at the other sheets that were coming out of the fax machine. They all said the same thing. The man was in love with her sister, there was absolutely no doubt in her mind. She saw Fiona scribble a message on the back of one of the sheets and place it into position. "What are you doing?"

"Answering." But the parade of pages wouldn't stop long enough for her to break the connection and send her reply. Frustrated, she headed for the door.

"Now where?" Bridgette called after her.

"I've got to go see him," was all she said before she ran outside.

And see him she did.

Because Hank was parked right in front of her house. When he saw her, he quickly got out of the car. He wasn't sure if she was bolting again.

Blocking her way to the van, he asked, "Well?"

What was he doing here? "My machine is spitting out your faxes. How did you—"

He nodded toward the curb and his car. "My cell phone, hooked up to my portable fax." He grinned. "Technology is a wonderful thing. I figured since we met because of a fax, maybe I could get you back that way."

He'd answered her question; now it was Fiona's

turn to answer his. "You still haven't answered my question."

Sunshine and roses filled her. She couldn't explain it any better than that. "It wasn't a question, it was a command."

"A plea," he corrected. "The downside about a fax is that you can't hear the person's voice. If you had, you would have known that it wasn't a command or an order, it was a plea." He knew he had to backtrack and start over. "Fiona, I'm—"

"Sorry," they both said at the same time, then laughed.

When they both began talking at the same time, Hank held up his hand. Eschewing niceties, he wanted his day in court before he lost precious ground.

"Me first. Fiona, I don't know what's going on in that head of yours, but I am not into just looks. I was, once, as my sister so obligingly pointed out, but no more than anyone is." He pinned her with a look that was at once loving and firm. "No more than you. Admit it, what first attracted you to me was my looks."

It wasn't just his looks, it was a myriad of things, things he'd referred to as chemistry. "Yes, but—"

"Okay, and my butt," he allowed with a grin. "Want to know what attracted me to you?"

She wasn't sure if she was ready for this. "What?"

"Same thing. Looks." Fiona sighed in response, but he wasn't about to recant. "You have got the greatest legs I've ever seen, even better than my first filly.'' He winked at her, sending ripples through her system. ''And as far as I was concerned, the rest of the package was just as good.''

She began to protest, then thought better of it. Bridgette's warning rang in her ears.

''In case you haven't noticed, I go for the total package. You're funny, sweet, and you turn me inside out when you look at me with those sexy eyes of yours. I don't want just looks, Fiona, I want the total package, the woman you've learned to become while everyone else was trying to figure out how to make their eyes look bigger with the right application of eyeliner and mascara.'' He took her into his arms, aware that several curtains along the block, as well as in her own house, had been drawn back and that they had an audience. He didn't care. ''I just want you to leave one thing out of the deal.''

''What?''

''Your insecurity.'' He pressed a kiss to her forehead. ''Because more than anyone else I've ever known, you have nothing to be insecure about. So, what do you say?'' He pulled her back so he could look into her eyes. ''*Will* you marry me?''

''Depends.''

He raised an eyebrow. ''On what?''

''Do I have to cater the wedding?''

He laughed, hugging her. ''No, we'll give you the day off. But I would like you to wear these under the wedding dress.'' As she watched, curious, Hank produced a pair of fishnet stockings out of his pocket and held them up in the air.

Fiona laughed as she snatched them from him. What more could she ask for than a man who was romantic enough to remember the first thing he'd said to make her tingle? "I love you."

He tilted her head back with the tip of his finger on her chin. "Does that mean the answer's yes?"

Her eyes smiled at him even as she did. "It was from the first minute I saw you."

He kissed her then, because words failed him for once. Kissed her because that was all he'd been thinking about since he'd walked out of her house one week, two days, five hours and thirty-one minutes ago.

Kissed her because he knew he'd go crazy if he didn't.

"By the way," he whispered as he pulled his head back.

"Hmm?" Beauty was not in the eyes of the beholder, she realized, it was a feeling. And she had it. She felt beautiful.

His lips passed over her face ever so lightly, drawing Fiona further into a vortex of emotion. "You don't need all that makeup to make you look gorgeous, you already are."

On her toes, she brought her body up against his. "Did I tell you I loved you?"

He inclined his head, his words flirting with her lips. "You might have mentioned it."

"Well, I do." She loved him so much, it hurt.

"That's good," he said, bringing his mouth down to hers, "because I'd hate to be in love all by myself."

"That," she assured him as she closed the gap, "will never happen again."

*   *   *   *   *

Look for Kent's story in
COWBOYS ARE FOR LOVING,
coming in July only from
Silhouette Desire®.

SILHOUETTE
DESIRE®

COMING NEXT MONTH

A MONTANA MAN Jackie Merritt

Man of the Month

Clint Barrow had lived for his son and the land—until Sierra came into his life. All he knew was her name—and that he wanted her. But when her memory returned, would he lose his mystery woman?

THE PATERNITY FACTOR Caroline Cross

Single father Shane Wyatt had just been told that his two-year-old daughter was not his by blood. Now he didn't trust *anyone*—not with his precious child, and certainly not with his heart—until Jessy Ross came along!

HIS SEDUCTIVE REVENGE Susan Crosby

Lone Wolves

Gabriel Marquez wanted revenge, and to do it he needed to seduce society princess Cristina Chandler, before she became engaged to another man. But the tough loner was unprepared for Cristina seducing him back!

THE RESTLESS VIRGIN Peggy Moreland

The McCloud Brides

One look at sexy Nash Rivers, and Samantha McCloud knew her long wait for the perfect man was over! But could the restless virgin persuade this rugged hunk to give her a lifetime of loving?

THE LITTLEST MARINE Maureen Child

Bachelor Battalion

After a wildly passionate night with marine Harding Casey, Elizabeth Stone found out she was pregnant just before he left to go overseas. He offered to do the honourable thing, but was it just for the baby's sake?

SEDUCTION OF THE RELUCTANT BRIDE
Barbara McCauley

Sam McCants knew he must be mad to agree to a two-month marriage to Faith Courtland. She had barely said 'I do' when she headed for the hills. But Sam was determined to find her—and have his wedding night!

COMING NEXT MONTH FROM
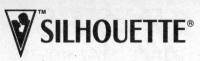
™ SILHOUETTE®

Sensation
A thrilling mix of passion, adventure and drama

A PERFECT HERO Paula Detmer Riggs
IF A MAN ANSWERS Merline Lovelace
AN INNOCENT MAN Margaret Watson
NOT WITHOUT RISK Suzanne Brockmann

Intrigue
Danger, deception and desire

NEVER CRY WOLF Patricia Rosemoor
ONLY A MEMORY AWAY Madeline St. Claire
REMEMBER MY TOUCH Gayle Wilson
PRIORITY MALE Susan Kearney

Special Edition
Compelling romances packed with emotion

TEMPORARY DADDY Jennifer Mikels
HEART OF THE HUNTER Lindsay McKenna
A HERO FOR SOPHIE JONES Christine Rimmer
A FAMILY KIND OF GUY Lisa Jackson
EVERY COWGIRL'S DREAM Arlene James
DIAGNOSIS: DADDY Jule McBride

HELEN R. MYERS

Come Sundown

In the steamy heat of Parish, Mississippi, there is a new chief of police. Ben Rader is here to shape up the department, and first on the list is the investigation of a mysterious death.

But things are not what they appear to be. Come Sundown things change in Parish…

FREE!

4 Books
and a surprise gift!

We would like to take this opportunity to thank you for reading this Silhouette® book by offering you the chance to take FOUR more specially selected titles from the Desire™ series absolutely FREE! We're also making this offer to introduce you to the benefits of the Reader Service™—

- ★ FREE home delivery
- ★ FREE gifts and competitions
- ★ FREE monthly Newsletter
- ★ Books available before they're in the shops
- ★ Exclusive Reader Service discounts

Accepting these FREE books and gift places you under no obligation to buy; you may cancel at any time, even after receiving your free shipment. Simply complete your details below and return the entire page to the address below. *You don't even need a stamp!*

YES! Please send me 4 free Desire books and a surprise gift. I understand that unless you hear from me, I will receive 6 superb new titles every month for just £2.70 each, postage and packing free. I am under no obligation to purchase any books and may cancel my subscription at any time. The free books and gift will be mine to keep in any case.

D9EB

Ms/Mrs/Miss/Mr ....Initials ....

Surname.. BLOCK CAPITALS PLEASE

Address..

....

....Postcode ....

Send this whole page to:
THE READER SERVICE, FREEPOST CN81, CROYDON, CR9 3WZ
(Eire readers please send coupon to: P.O. Box 4546, DUBLIN 24.)